BLOOD
✦✦✦✦✦✦✦ ON ✦✦✦✦✦✦✦
SATAN'S CLAW
O R,
The Devil's Skin

BLOOD
✦✦✦✦✦✦✦✦ ON ✦✦✦✦✦✦✦✦
SATAN'S CLAW
O R,
The Devil's Skin

ROBERT WYNNE-SIMMONS
With illustrations by Richard Wells

unbound

First published in 2022

Unbound
Level 1, Devonshire House, One Mayfair Place, London W1J 8AJ
www.unbound.com

Text design by Ellipsis, Glasgow

A CIP record for this book is available from the British Library

ISBN 978-1-78965-158-4 (hardback)
ISBN 978-1-78965-157-7 (ebook)

Printed in Great Britain by CPI Group (UK)

1 3 5 7 9 8 6 4 2

Foreword

Blood on Satan's Claw. I first watched it on VHS, at a friend's house, one night when I was fifteen or sixteen. My friend, Stuart, who had a father who worked in Spain as a diplomat, came back one day with the film in his attaché case. We watched all the films he brought back without complaint, because Stuart's dad *always* came up with the goods, albeit sometimes goods that were third- or fourth-generation copies.

That night our jaws dropped. To this day, that feeling of not quite knowing what kind of film we watched is something I've not had since, but we knew that something *different*, something *other* was playing out before us.

Satan's Claw, we were told several decades later, was one of the main trunks of the tree that we now know as 'folk horror', alongside *Witchfinder General* (dir. Michael

Reeves, 1968) and *The Wicker Man* (dir. Robin Hardy, 1973). But back then, it was just a *brilliant* horror film with no other labels attached. And it was one of the best horror films we had ever watched. We would talk about the film non-stop and it became a Friday-night staple.

As you grow up and leave those formative years behind, you want to read about the films you love and admire; you discover essays written about them, are told about those films, and you get to meet the people who starred in those films. I had the honour of curating the film six years ago or so for my 'Johnny's House of Horror' season at Plymouth University, and we invited Linda Hayden down to the Ocean City. I sat next to her as we watched the film on the big screen. It was one of the most surreal moments of my life. But then I got to talk to her about her experience on the film and the screen-play and I found that by exploring her experiences, I was no longer just watching a horror film, I was connecting with something deeper, and it started with the person who sat down at their typewriter all those years ago and began to tell a story. A story that persists, and continues to be talked about and discovered.

That storyteller is Robert Wynne-Simmons.

For me, the definition of folk horror is the upper-class demonisation of lower/working classes. And the lower class believing what they are fed and then spreading those lies around them and their families like a virus so families will attack families and distrust will be sown until all is destroyed apart from the original tellers of the lie. Because why would the higher-ups *ever* lie to us?

With this book, Robert confirms those whispers in the wind, but lays the foundations for them, and gives us a story that is, for me at least, infinitely better than the original film. It's the unshakable belief of religion, the unbreakable power of law, of being better than someone beneath you but having to go along with the fairy tale of common workers having a superstition about something (otherwise they can rise up and usurp your power!), only to find out that the superstition is real, tangible and connected to everyone's faith and that the existential void of hopelessness that the superstition creates when they try their hardest to cling on to whatever 'god' they believe in will be able to destroy them all.

The Devil's Skin has some perfect moments in it. The writing; I don't think I've read writing this fine since I first discovered horror, and I love every bloody sentence of it.

Take these two examples, one uncanny, one gruesome:

Get thee behind me, Satan!' he muttered aloud through his teeth, but even as he did so, he began to regret his words. All at once the night seemed to darken, and he could feel someone following close behind him. He knew who it was, and as he walked on, he could even sense the hot breath on the back of his neck. He dared not turn round, but walked straight ahead . . .

And a little further along:

He lifted it gingerly with his fingertips, revealing a cheekbone, then a bony face, half-covered by the earth, a worm crawling on an eye, which was staring straight up at him. It was not a human face, although it was hard to say what it was, and the eye was still moist in the skull as if alive. Even though it didn't blink, it appeared as if it might. But it had no lid. Instead it looked right into him with a terrible intensity. The immediate effect of this hideous vision was only momentary, as he dropped the rotten wood in terror and ran away as fast as he could, tumbling helplessly over the newly heaped earth. But as he ran, the memory of the eye stayed with him.

Robert's use of language is powerful, connecting you to the ancient storytellers who didn't care about being flowery or important. They just wanted to tell a tale that gripped you from the first page to the last. With this book, Robert has done the job admirably; *The Devil's Skin* adds another layer of contextuality to *The Blood on Satan's Claw* and has created a work that can be read and appreciated on its own but also as a companion piece to the film.

This is no mere tie-in: this is a formidable work of literature in its own right. It rattles along at an incredible pace and is wholly entertaining, yet it unfolds as an unflinching portrayal of those that live hard life on the land, their connections with religion, superstition and terror of what lies beneath. I'm privileged to have been one of the first readers of this formidable work, and now you, through the uncanny Unbound, are about to dip in. I must thank Robert Wynne-Simmons for this wholly satisfying book and also Richard Wells for bringing his artistic genius to it. They are a perfect match.

Johnny Mains
Plymouth
March 2022

Introduction

Revisiting the world of *Blood on Satan's Claw* or *The Devil's Skin* has been a fascinating voyage of discovery. I found that the characters were still alive, and had even mellowed over the years. Writing a novel about them allowed me time to reflect on their motivations and background, to go beyond the film and see something more of their secret lives. I was also led to explore other places in the dark world of Chapel Folding, as I have now called the village where the film is set, and into new scenes which I have now written for the first time.

In addition to the village, many of the characters in the film did not have names, but I discovered a number of pencilled notes in the margin of my screenplay and have used these to give names to such characters as the Judge, the Squire and the Doctor. The novel seemed to demand this, in order to create a complete world from which the events of the film were taken.

The screenplay of the film now known as *The Blood on Satan's Claw* was written to a very tight schedule, made necessary because Pinewood Studios had already been booked for a fixed date, 1 April 1970, by the production company, Chilton Films (for Tigon British). I was originally asked to write a portmanteau screenplay, comprised of three distinct half-hour films. Although this format was fashionable at the time, I much preferred the idea of a full-length feature, so I set my stories in one village with some characters overlapping, to make that possible. I wrote the first draft in three weeks with the suggestion that it should be made as a continuous feature film, and the producers were soon won round to the idea. But by then there were only six weeks left before shooting was due to begin. This meant that the final screenplay, which bore the title *The Devil's Skin*, was barely ready in time.

I was supported in my decision by the director who was then nominated, Piers Haggard, but because of the timescale there were still certain problems which could not easily be overcome. The actors, who had to be booked well in advance, were booked as for the three-story version, and some of them had other commitments and could not move their dates around. When the film was made, Piers was happy that I should be there as part of the team, as last-minute alterations were sometimes necessary. He did an excellent job in keeping the story flowing, and holding the attention of his audience so that they did not notice any anomalies, but anomalies there inevitably were.

In 2021, fifty years after the film's release, I felt that the time had come to celebrate its continued success as one of the founding films of 'folk horror' by bringing out a definitive version of the full story in novel form, free of some of the pressures under which the film itself was made.

To those who have not seen the film, I hope this book will give a taste of the very special atmosphere which the film possessed, so they may be encouraged to view it when they have the chance. I also hope that this novel itself may be able to survive the test of time, as the film has done, and stand up in the future in its own right.

Robert Wynne-Simmons

Chapter One

The Interests of the Reverend Fallowfield

he Reverend Lucian Fallowfield was a simple man, or that was how he liked to see himself. When asked about his religious beliefs, he would answer, 'I am a gentle Puritan.' That was why, when, by chance, he was offered a living in the country, in a place called Chapel Folding, the very name of it immediately appealed to him. A Protestant monarch was safely on the throne of England, Scotland and Ireland, and the threat of Catholicism had passed. The religious wars, which he had found so distasteful, were now at an end. Buried in the countryside, in a simple parish, he could put all that savagery behind him. The roars of the hell-fire preachers would no longer ring in his ears, and the stench of the last witch-burning would no longer remain in his nostrils. He could breathe pure fresh air in the open countryside, and whenever he thought of Chapel Folding he imagined a small, whitewashed chapel, such as Saint Francis of Assisi might have built, surrounded by fields of wheat and barley. There, like Saint Francis, he would be able to communicate with the birds of the air and the beasts of the field, and find peace and godliness.

The reality was, of course, not exactly as he had imagined. The fields were there, as he had pictured them, but they formed a small oasis among dense woods and hills. The village had been difficult for him to find, as there were no signposts, and the roads were winding and muddy. Also, there was no chapel. Instead, there was an old, imposing church with a tower, but it stood aloof from the rest of the community as if it did not belong. The village, which was mostly made up of large interconnecting farms and their cottages, had turned its back on the church, probably because the original houses had crumbled away following the Black Death, and nobody had liked to build there since. He had thought that the church would be at the centre of the community, but it felt neglected and was poorly preserved. As a new and inexperienced vicar of the parish, the curious position of its church reinforced his own sense of being an outsider. Nevertheless, he soon had the old vestry whitewashed, and turned into a schoolroom for the local children. He was a strong believer in the openness and innocence of childhood, and although he could see in his congregation quite a few angry old curmudgeons, fixed in their dark ways, he had hopes that he could transform the village through its offspring, and he told them so in his sermons.

At first his classes had been poorly attended, but over time, in ones and twos, new children joined him, when their parents decided that it was safe to let their sons and daughters be taught by this Puritanical stranger. It surprised him how little their children knew about the basic story of the gospels, and how confused they were about Christianity in general.

'John the Baptist used to drown people in the river, until they caught him and chopped his head off!' said one little boy, gleefully.

Before he arrived in Chapel Folding, Fallowfield had been warned by the bishop that in some of these rural communities the people were barely Christian at all. He had not believed it at first, but then he began to understand what the bishop meant.

At the end of the working day, after the last pupil had gone home, and the sunlight was slowly swallowed by the surrounding woodland, he would often linger outside the church and look up at its castellated tower, from the corners of which small stone figures were grinning down at him. As the bats flew out at twilight, circling around them, they grew more alive, and on days when the children had been most obtuse, it seemed as if they were deliberately mocking all his attempts at achieving his Puritan ideals. Although gargoyles were very common throughout England, he wondered why it was that they were ever put up there, on top of a Christian building. What could the stonemasons who carved them have been thinking? Had no-one realised how inappropriate they were? And what were they? That also fascinated him. His personal theory was that they represented the old discredited local gods, which should have been banished years ago. What possible need could a Christian church have to be guarded by these dwarfish, hideous and misshapen stone soldiers?

There was one gargoyle in particular that he detested, without really knowing why. It looked like a vicious grinning bat with a hollow face on which cobwebs had grown, and it was to be found not only on the tower, but on bosses in the vaulting inside the church itself, as if it belonged there. Had he the funds, he would have had these little pagan devils removed, but they were in such inaccessible places that he couldn't easily reach them with a chisel, and he knew that if he tried to persuade anybody to do the job for him, he would quickly become very unpopular. People were unnaturally fond of these little demons, it seemed, and after a while, even Fallowfield himself got used to them.

The Reverend Fallowfield loved to go on walks, which was considered a strange practice, as no villager ever went on a walk unless they had a particular destination in mind. Consequently, he did not have to go far before he ventured into areas of tangled woodland which many of his parishioners had never visited in all their lives. It was on one of these lonely walks, which were so frowned upon, that he sprained his ankle on some broken stones hidden in the undergrowth. He sat down in pain and looked around, wondering where the path had gone, and soon realised that he had lost his way completely. He took time to allow the pain to subside a little and take in his wild surroundings, full of brambles and ivy. He noticed that part of an overgrown wall, made of the same stones as those on which he had fallen, stood nearby. He hobbled forward and could see that the wall did not stand alone, but formed part of a very old, ruined chapel. He began to imagine that he had discovered the original 'Chapel Folding', the existence of which everyone in the village had vigorously denied. But there it was, a chapel, even though there was very little left of it. In front of its arched doorway stood an ancient monolith, a big rough stone, stained with lichen, and evidently much older than the chapel itself. The chapel arch behind was so thick with ivy that it appeared at first to be made of it. He pushed his way towards it through the thicket and peered inside.

This ruined building was the total opposite of the idealised chapel he had once imagined when he thought of Chapel Folding. It was sullen and unwelcoming, as if it did not want intruders, and him least of all. As he scrambled through the arch, he felt soft drops descending on his head, and wiped away some dark, unpleasant liquid, like the excretion of hidden beetles. The ground was covered with blackened creepers and angry thorns which threatened to draw blood, and in the centre was a burnt-out area, as if a fire had recently been lit. He touched the blackened leaves, expecting them to disintegrate into ash, but it seemed they had not been burnt, and were simply black by nature. Something moved through them, which made him shudder and draw back. He wasn't wanted there. He was certain of it. It was not a house of God. He scrambled out as soon as he could, and resolved to tell nobody about it. Either they already knew about it, or they should not know.

As he limped back towards the village, he passed an old wooden shack which belonged to one man who did know a great deal about the history of Chapel Folding. His name was Ned Carter, a charcoal-burner who lived alone on the edge of the woods and had little to do with the rest of the village, most of whom thought him mad. Fallowfield had first encountered Ned on a previous walk, and discovered him to be a fountain of knowledge when it came to local history and folklore. He even saw in this isolated man in his battered hat some sort of kindred spirit, and although, despite constant badgering, he had never been able to persuade Ned to attend evensong in his church, the two of them had become unlikely friends. He was the only person prepared to talk openly about the magic rituals and the 'strange goings-on' for which Folding had once been notorious. Fallowfield sat down on a log which Ned had fashioned into a bench, and rested his swollen ankle, while Ned brought him a battered pewter mug filled with some bitter herbal infusion of which he did not like to ask the name.

'Have you ever wandered up that way, Ned?' said Fallowfield, indicating the stretch of pathless wilderness where he had got lost and stumbled upon the hidden chapel. He wanted to introduce the topic, without directly mentioning it.

'No, I'm never been up there,' was Ned's reply, which was oddly negative, as Ned had been most places at one time or another, looking everywhere for dry wood. Why not there?

'Do you know anyone who does go up there?'

'Nope.'

That might have been the end of it, had not Ned added, after some consideration, 'Exceptin'...'

'Who?'

'Exceptin' I've seen some children goin' up there once in a while, to play their games.'

This was most unexpected.

'Why would children go up there, and what games?'

'They go most everywhere,' said Ned, with a shrug, but the Reverend would not let up. Were they his children from the school who went up there? He would not like it if they were. Ned could not be sure. Perhaps they were some gypsy children, or from another village? Ned had no idea and looked even a little alarmed that the Reverend was being so persistent. Eventually, finding himself completely blocked, Fallowfield asked if Ned had something with which he could bandage his ankle, as he had damaged it on some stones by a ruin in the wood.

'What stones?' asked Ned.

'I think it was part of a wall.'

'There's naught up that way that I knows of,' said Ned, and Lucian Fallowfield could see that he was not prepared to change that opinion, even when confronted by the evidence of a sprained ankle. He seemed to doubt the real cause of the accident. Tree stumps, maybe, not stones.

'They're thinking of ploughing up Tarrant's Field,' Ned suddenly remarked, changing the subject, as he fetched a stained old piece of cloth and a wooden splint. 'No good'll come of it.'

'I expect not,' said the vicar, with an indulgent smile. He knew about Ned's fears. Jack Tarrant was a local anti-hero about whom Ned knew a whole heap of unpleasant stories, each one of which tended to contradict the last. In one story he was a highwayman who had refused to die when hung and had pronounced a curse on the whole village while the rope was still round his neck, and he hanging from it. In another, his long life of crime had made him hugely rich, and people would search everywhere for his money, even though they became fatally ill if they found a penny of it. In another version, the villagers had become so afraid of him that, when he died, they cut his body into a thousand tiny pieces and scattered it all across the field that bore his name. In yet other stories he wasn't human at all, but a goblin or a ghost, like Jack o' Lantern, Jack o' the Green, and all the other Jacks that people spoke about in whispers. All these stories had a common ending. Jack Tarrant was buried somewhere in the place known as Tarrant's Field, and had put a curse on it, and out of superstition no-one dared to touch it. It had put the vicar in mind of the potter's field, where Judas Iscariot had met his end.

Strange plants grew in Tarrant's Field, and in early spring snakes from the woodland would wind their way through its long, unkempt grasses. But despite this, the Reverend Fallowfield had often visited it himself. He found it had a curious beauty all its own, and was even rather magical. He didn't share Ned's fear of the place, or its snakes, and he told him so. Ned said no more, quietly disappearing back into his shed.

Recently the spinster Isobel Banham had acquired this rough old meadow after the last owner had died. She was reluctant to touch it because of the superstitions which surrounded it, but Squire Middleton, who was always a busybody and, so Fallowfield believed, possessed a strongly atheistic tendency, kept pushing her to do something with it. It was an eyesore, he said. He couldn't bear to see good land going to waste if there was money to be made from it. Fallowfield, on the other hand, would be very sad to see the destruction of his little wilderness.

There was no love lost between the practical squire and the secretive vicar, and so it greatly surprised the Reverend

Fallowfield when, shortly after his talk with Ned Carter, he received an invitation from Edgar Middleton to join him at the manor house to share a bottle of fine port and discuss some matters of importance to the village. Squire Middleton had been deeply suspicious of the Puritanical vicar ever since he first arrived, and had maintained his suspicions over the years, long after Fallowfield had become accepted by the rest of the parish. He had often hinted at a quality of dubious zealotry in the man, which made him feel very uncomfortable. Now he suddenly wanted to share a bottle of port with him. Fallowfield should have been more wary.

The manor house was a ramshackle place, hardly worthy of the name, and in the evening light it appeared to crumble into the ground. Its owner, however, was a proud man, who behaved as if he owned the whole village and estates as least twice as big as they really were. He welcomed Fallowfield with a hearty handshake, which demonstrated that, although now rather portly, he was still a strong man and would take no nonsense from anyone. He ushered him inside.

The vicar looked around at the sagging, oak-beamed room. A generous fire was burning in the grate, and there on a small table was the bottle of port, glimmering red, and two glasses. Cold meats of all kinds were arranged on the heavy sideboard. On the opposite wall hung the Squire's collection of muskets and rifles, some long and thin, others which opened out like trumpets, lined up one above the other. The Squire was fond of hunting, although whenever asked what he liked to hunt, the answer was always the same.

'Poachers,' he would bellow, with a chuckle.

The Reverend Fallowfield seated himself cautiously in these new surroundings.

'I have had complaints,' said the Squire, 'from the parents of children at your school.'

'Complaints?' Fallowfield was taken off guard. He found it hard to believe. He thought things were running swimmingly. The children were learning fast. They loved his Christian tales.

'Yes, complaints. You have been telling the children stories. Many are now suffering from nightmares.'

'What stories?'

'I hardly like to say.'

Middleton was no longer the magnanimous squire who had issued the invitation, but had very quickly transformed into the bullying magistrate. Fallowfield felt sick in his stomach.

'I have told them nothing which would cause nightmares. There must be another reason.'

'Oh, yes? What reason?' The Squire waited for the vicar to confess to something, but no confession came.

'I teach them the tenets of Christianity,' he said. It sounded pompous, but Fallowfield would not give way.

'Two young girls were overheard telling some depraved story, which they said was from the Bible.'

Fallowfield, who had begun to sip his port, put down the glass. 'I don't believe it. Tell me who they were.'

The Squire did not reply. After a pause, he said,

'You know the story of Lot and his two daughters?'

'Of course I know it, but I would never tell it, not to children.'

'I think you'll agree that in a rural community where incest is not unknown, it ventures a little near the bone.'

'I never tell such tales, even from the Bible.'

'And stories about local horrors, stories we never tell here. You have been deliberately frightening them.'

'What stories?'

'Stories about Jack Tarrant, for instance. Where did you hear these stories? You have been nosing about. I have learnt never to trust men who appear too holy, Reverend. They're always hiding something nasty.'

Fallowfield felt the blood draining from his face.

'Furthermore, it is my opinion that you have too close a relationship with some of the girls in your class. Not that I can blame you. Since my wife died, I have been on the lookout myself, and there are some nice young fillies in the village that I wouldn't mind riding, but you are a priest, and you should be more careful.'

'How could you suggest such a thing?!'

'Then what is this I hear about you and Angela Blake?'

This truly shocked the sensitive vicar. Angela, or 'Angel' as she was often called, was one of his best pupils, intelligent and eager to learn, and he had responded to that eagerness, but the Squire was suggesting something quite other. Fallowfield rose to his feet, ashen-faced, and appeared to be looking around for some receptacle in which to vomit.

'I don't know what you think of me, but this is all untrue!'

'Oh, God, can you not take a joke, man? She's a pretty girl. You should have learnt by now not to be so damned pious. People here don't like it. Your predecessor was an old man, but he still enjoyed strong ale, and in his youth he could out-dance anyone in the village. He was popular for that, particularly with the ladies. Ah, but you Puritans never dance.'

The Reverend Fallowfield could take no more. He had his hat on and was out the door. It was dark and moonless outside, and without a lantern the road back to the rectory was long enough. He was aware, as he walked away, of the puffed-up figure of the Squire, now silhouetted in the yellow light of his doorway, watching him go. The small stocky figure called out, 'You be careful! People notice things!'

At this Fallowfield quickened his step. The door closed, and all was darkness.

As he walked home, he had time to collect his thoughts. He decided that everything the Squire had said, except perhaps about the children's nightmares, was a complete lie, intended to humiliate him. The Squire was a profane man, and since the death of his dragon of a wife, his 'greasy Joan' as he liked to call her, he had become more profane than ever. How dare he fling accusations and insinuations at his innocent pupils, and particularly Angel Blake!

Of course he cared for Angel Blake. She came from a very sad and unpromising background, but she was highly intelligent and bright as a button. Her father was a rough farm labourer, a surly, stupid man, and aggressive with it. He had been in the way of hitting his long-suffering wife, who had tragically died when Angel was only seven, of a food poisoning, from which all of Dr Grubb's emetics could not save her. Despite all this, you would never guess from the pretty fair-haired girl who so eagerly attended his classes that she had suffered so much.

A wind was getting up, and the trees had begun to wave their arms about like tethered giants. He must get home before the rain. As he walked on through the dark windy dell, he thought of the 'valley of the shadow of death', which was what the night seemed to have suddenly become, yet in the darkness, he could see Angel's face, those beautiful eyes, and the innocent way she looked at him. How could the Squire defile such a child with his crude insinuations? But then, was the Squire telling him something about himself, something that he should know? Was he hiding something? Was it love he felt for that girl? Or worse? No! Such a terrible thought.

'Get thee behind me, Satan!' he muttered aloud through his teeth, but even as he did so, he began to regret his words. All at once the night seemed to darken, and he could feel someone following close behind him. He knew who it was, and as he walked on, he could even sense the hot breath on the back of his neck. He dared not turn round, but walked straight ahead, and did not deviate once in all the rest of his journey, until the rectory door was safely closed behind him, and the rains began.

At last, he could relax in his simple bedroom, with its dark wooden cross on the pure white wall. There he was safe. As was his custom, he reached for the consolation of his big black Bible, and opened it at random, reading what he found there and taking the thought with him into his sleep. He hit upon the Book of Ezekiel, chapter 37, and read these words:

'And as I prophesied, there was a noise, and behold a shaking, and the bones came together, bone to his bone. And when I beheld, Lo, the sinews came up upon them, and the skin covered them above, but there was no breath in them . . .'

Outside, the naked branches of a tree, whipped up by the wind, had begun to rattle at his bedroom window like the skin and bones of the dead.

In the loneliness of his large manor house, the Squire could also hear the wild and insistent tapping of the trees, and as he turned over in his lumpy bed, he reached out for the comfort of his 'greasy Joan', the one person who had given order to his life, but could not find her. It was a fearsome night.

Chapter Two

✦ ✦ ✦

I Curse the Day I Ploughed in Tarrant's Field

It was a bright clear dawn in early March when Ralph Gower harnessed his horses to the plough. He did so at first light because there was much work to be done that day. The breath of his two great shire horses clouded in the morning air. He was a strong young man, and proud of his abilities as a workman. There was good money to be made, so he understood, for the ploughing up of Tarrant's Field, and he was the man to do it. He had worked for several of the local farms as a hired hand, and he knew the temper of the dark soil of Chapel Folding as well as anyone. But he preferred to work for the elderly and sometimes temperamental Isobel Banham, and there was a good reason for that. Her name was Cathy Vespers, the delicate and lively daughter of Ellen Vespers, Isobel's personal maid.

She was still quite young and a pupil at the church school, but her bright and insatiable curiosity was the perfect foil for his very practical, if sometimes rather pedestrian, way of thinking, and he adored her. His lack of too much imagination and his total focus on the matter in hand meant that all the superstitions surrounding Tarrant's Field were of no concern to him. He alone would tackle it. He was quite fearless in many things, and Cathy was proud of him for that.

He had no memory of ever having proposed marriage to Cathy, but when she had announced one day that it was what was going to happen in a few years' time, he hadn't argued. After all, it was also what he himself had always longed and hoped for. Their only problem was a lack of money, and the ploughing of Tarrant's Field would put a few more shillings in the earthenware jar he had hidden behind a beam at home, and bring a little nearer the day when he and Cathy could announce their intentions to the world.

As he wiped his hands free of grease, and tested the strength of the harness, he looked up, as he always did, at the sky and at the weather. The sky had taken on an ethereal blue, and gulls and crows were circling above him. He noticed there were clouds banking on the horizon, and this worried him, as it was a condition of his payment that the work should all be completed within a day. The horses also sensed the threat of the gathering clouds, which by their shadow had given to the whole scene a supernatural light. They were more restless than he had ever known them to be, snorting and stamping at the ground with their big shaggy hooves. It came as a relief when he felt the ploughshare dig into the fresh earth, and the plough move forward with a shudder. The grasses broke apart and the black soil rose and fell back again as the fresh cut was made. Fortunately, the recent rains meant that the ground parted easily, and although there were large stones and stumps which occasionally brought him to a halt, for the most part the going was easy, and he prided himself on the regularity of the dark furrows that he now laid out.

'Ralph,' a voice was calling, 'Ralph!' It was Cathy, running with a satchel on her back, on her way to school. She had called by to give him encouragement in his day's task. He took off his hat and waved it, wiping the sweat from his brow. He told her it was going well. For a while she followed him along the edge of the field. His work seemed lighter when he knew she was there, even though they did not exchange a word, and so he felt a little sad when she had to climb the stile and follow the path down towards the church, and he was alone again. All the same he remained cheerful, as the day was still young, and he felt strong in himself as he steadied his plough.

After he had been working for some time, the weather became warmer, surprisingly so for the time of year, and the flagon of beer which he had brought with him could do little to assuage his growing thirst. His muscles began to feel the strain. The field had appeared to grow in size as he reached the swollen belly of it, but he was determined not to be defeated. Attracted by the newly exposed earth, a number of crows were collecting, flopping from place to place as they examined and pecked at the moist ground. One or two flew very close to him, almost landing on his shoulder. Others watched him sideways as he worked. Then suddenly there was a fierce cry, and a single bird swooped straight down out of the sky. Ralph let go of the plough and started round to see a group of birds pecking at something in the furrows behind him. A bone was projecting through the earth, barely noticeable at first, but enough to arouse his curiosity. The birds flew away as he approached, and with growing alarm he discovered they had been pecking at pieces of fur, blood and torn flesh spread out on the ground. Had he unwittingly killed and ploughed through some hibernating animal? Some of the birds now began to return. Ralph became aware that a shape was hidden beneath a small, blackened branch which lay near to where he stood. He lifted it gingerly with his fingertips, revealing a cheekbone, then a cavernous face, half-covered by the earth, with a worm crawling on one eye, which was staring straight up at him. It was never a human face, although it was hard to say what it was, and the eye was still moist in the skull as if alive. Even though it didn't blink, it appeared as if it might. But it had no lid. Instead, it looked right into him with a terrible intensity.

The immediate effect of this hideous vision was only momentary, as he dropped the rotten wood in terror and ran away as fast as he could, tumbling helplessly over the newly heaped earth. But as he ran, the memory of the eye stayed with him. He reached the edge of the field, bent double and breathing fast, uncertain what to do. Even as he looked at the small company of birds gathered near his plough, and the others circling round, he could hardly believe what he had seen. What animal was it, and was it still alive? He felt as if some living being had looked right into him and entered his soul. It was no animal, he decided. He had seen something which no mortal man should see, and he would pay a price.

He felt dizzy and confused. He couldn't think which way to turn. His instinct told him not to go to the farmhouse straight away, as he wouldn't be believed, and might be beaten for his trouble, particularly so if he had left the horses behind. Cathy had told him that there was a stranger at the farm, a learned man, she said. Ralph had a great respect and fear for learned men, having never himself encountered one. He was convinced that they were all magicians, and could he ever trust such a man? His punishment might be all the more severe.

But then again what choice did he have? Who would listen to him? He thought of his old mother, ill in bed at home, and knew she might collapse completely if he told her what he had seen. She was deadly afraid of such things. On the other hand, he could never keep such a discovery secret for long, and if it was a threat to the village, it was his duty not to do so.

A large hand on a dark dining table was crumpling up a napkin and supporting the weight of a man who rose slowly from his seat. It was Isobel Banham's visitor, the Judge, a proud, imposing man, with a brooding, almost menacing manner. The room in which he stood was large and square, with dark oak beams and an air of beeswax polish. The furniture, which centred on the huge dining table, was grand, but had a certain rough-hewn quality which betrayed its country workmanship.

'You expect me to give credit to such village nonsense,' growled the Judge, 'and believe you saw these things with your own eyes? What is your name, young man?'

Ralph stood awkwardly by the door. He was flushed with embarrassment and unsteady in his speech.

'Ralph Gower, an't please you, sir. I wouldn't lie to your worship. Its face looked stark up at me from the furrows, as if it were only new dead.'

'And you work these fields each year?' said the Judge.

'Yes, sir, but not this one, not Tarrant's Field, but I thought nothing wrong, until I saw'm.'

'Ralph, you are disturbing me greatly,' interrupted Isobel. She was a woman of about sixty, thin, and nervous in her movements, with her fine hair turning grey, and was sitting at the side of the table, which was laid for three, although it could seat many more. Only the places of her and the Judge showed signs of a meal having been eaten. The other place setting was untouched. The Judge moved round behind her, as if to protect her from Ralph's alarming revelations.

'I don't mean it, ma'am,' he said.

'It won't go lightly with you, Ralph Gower, if this story be untrue,' said the Judge, 'but I have to confess 'tis several years since I had a murder discovered on my own doorstep!'

'But it weren't human, if you'll forgive me, sir. It were all torn to pieces, and there was fur.'

'Fur?' snorted the Judge, disappointed. 'Then it was an animal's remains!'

Ralph could see that the Judge was fast losing interest. At any moment he might be thrown out.

'No, sir, honest,' he stuttered, 'it was more like . . . some . . . fiend.' He knew, as soon as he said the word, that he should not have said it.

'You see, my dear Isobel, the way old tales and superstitions die hard among country folk,' said the Judge, contemptuously.

'Please come and see, your worship,' pleaded Ralph, not willing to give up, 'then you'll believe me.'

The Judge was silent for a moment.

'I believe, young man, as much as I am able,' he said at last. 'I know, for instance, that I have been disturbed in

27

the middle of an excellent meal, which I am reluctant to leave. Ellen always prepares the most delicious breakfast.'

But then it was Isobel who could hold herself back no longer.

'Pray, dear Nathan, do ascertain the truth of his disgusting story, if merely to set my mind at rest.'

The Judge smiled indulgently for the first time.

'You see, Ralph, how badly you have distressed your mistress. Very well, as you insist, we shall leave the pleasures of Ellen's country cooking and investigate your "fiend", and then I will prove to you, once and for all, that he doesn't exist.' With this Judge Nathan Mandeville donned his feathered hat and headed for the door.

'Come!' he said, and Ralph followed him.

Ralph followed very unwillingly, but he felt almost as frightened of the Judge as he was of what he had seen in the field. He was not being allowed to escape or recover from the shock, and this formidable man was hell-bent on forcing him to look once more at the most horrifying thing he had ever seen in his life. He hung back as much as he could, but the Judge was coming ever nearer to where his horses stood, and were strangely silent. The Judge prodded the ground with his stick.

'Where is it?' he snarled. Ralph's voice got caught in a lump in his throat, and he was unable to speak. As he looked at the newly turned earth, he was quite incapable of remembering where he had seen what he knew he had seen. It all looked completely different.

'It were just here, I swear,' he pleaded, when his voice finally returned. The Judge turned over the sod thoughtfully.

'A body? Human remains?'

'No, sir. I aren't never seen no human face the like.'

'A body, once buried, does not commonly retain much of its human aspect,' said the Judge, slowly, 'nor once unearthed does it commonly evaporate into thin air.'

Ralph, deeply embarrassed, continued to look around at the unyielding earth, hoping for some sign which might let him explain what he had seen, and where he had found it.

'I must surmise, Ralph,' thundered the Judge, 'that you have been wasting my time,' and Ralph immediately felt that to waste the time of such a man was not wise. The Judge walked up alone to the crest of the field, observing the entire area carefully, then wrapped his cloak about him and headed back towards the farm. Ralph followed silently, as if expecting to be whipped.

They had just reached the hedgerow at the field's edge when Ralph noticed a sudden movement in the grass. He could feel every hair on his body stand on end.

'Look, my lord,' he whispered. 'There's som'ert that's alive, over there!'

The Judge moved quickly towards the place that Ralph indicated and tossed up a snake with the end of his stick.

'It's only a snake,' he snorted.

From somewhere behind him, Ralph then heard another voice, which came as a shock, because he had seen no-one else in the meadow.

'There are quite a number in these parts,' said the Reverend Fallowfield. 'The milder weather brings them out.'

'You call this mild, sir?' said the Judge.

'Comparatively,' said Fallowfield, as he picked up the snake and stroked it gently. '*Ubique opera Domini*,' he added, as he observed it in more detail, coiling round his hand.

'The Reverend has been teaching the children at his school down by the church all about such things,' explained Ralph, as it seemed that Fallowfield was not going to introduce himself.

'Ah, the village pastor,' said the Judge. 'Perhaps you can throw some light on a strange matter. Gower here claims he discovered a severely deformed anatomy lying in the furrows. Do you know of anyone around here who was badly disfigured who might have gone missing recently, some kind of freak, an abnormality in nature?'

'Not since old Meg Parsons died,' said Fallowfield, 'but

we do find some strange people wandering through from time to time.'

'I expect so,' said the Judge, and walked away.

Chapter Three

The Spare Room

 find it worrying,' said the Judge later that afternoon, 'that an apparently honest young man could be driven, by fear and superstition, and in broad daylight, to see terrible things which simply are not there.'

'Ralph Gower has worked for me for years,' said Isobel with a sigh, 'and this is how he shows his gratitude, with these horrible lies.'

'I am not so sure he was lying. In his mind, he did see something.'

'You frighten me, Nathan.'

'We still have a deal of work to do before these foolish old beliefs are all stamped out. Superstition is like the ergot in the rye. It maddens whole villages.'

'I have very little to do with the village these days,' said Isobel, as if the Judge were pointing the finger at her. The Judge grunted and was silent but did not hide his general disapproval. Then he leant across the table and patted her hand protectively.

'Did you know, Isobel, that there are some people round here who claim that this very house is haunted?'

'It is very old, and folk are very imaginative,' she said, defensively.

'I overheard your maid saying that there was something in the walls that made strange noises. Is there? Rats, I presume?'

'I don't have rats. What Ellen encountered was not rats. It was very much bigger than that, so she said,' muttered Isobel, before she could stop herself. 'Ellen heard something in the spare room. I told her not to go poking around in there.'

'I sincerely hope,' said the Judge, fixing her with his dark and penetrating eyes, 'that you yourself do not believe her tales.'

'Of course not,' said Isobel, scornfully. She would have liked to add that it was hard to live in a place like Chapel Folding without being a little infected by the fears and beliefs which pervaded the air you breathed, but she knew how furious the Judge would be. She decided to change the subject.

'But I want to talk to you urgently, Nathan, about a quite different matter.'

'You mean about your nephew?' The Judge had

received prior warning of this, and knew that Isobel would be concerned.

'Peter, yes. You have always been so good to him, and I am very grateful for your good advice, but I have had a letter which deeply worries me. It is not in his usual style. He sounds agitated, and says he is coming here on Friday, that is today, and that he may bring someone with him. What is it that is so pressing?'

'I would not imagine, my dear, that it is anything to worry about.'

'But you have acted as his mentor.'

'In matters of law, and in his studies, but affairs of the heart are not my business.'

'But who is it, this person that he might bring? You must know.'

'I believe it is Rosalind Barton.'

'Barton?' She tightened up at the very mention of the name, her eyes becoming slits.

'Her family do not approve,' he said, consolingly.

'I imagine they do not. But I don't care a fig for what they might think. We must put a stop to this!' She had suspected there was bad news hidden behind Peter's friendly, if slightly anxious and very tentative, letter.

'My advice is not to interfere, but let it burn itself out. He is young, and he is entitled to a brief infatuation. He will learn.'

'I will not allow it!' said Isobel, bitterly. Nathan watched her carefully, and inwardly he gave a smile. He

liked to see her thwarted and angry. This was the spirited
Isobel he had known when he was young.

'We will see what we can do,' he said.

He was well aware that her nervous, petulant manner
hid a steel-hard core, which he secretly admired. It would
only show itself at times, and this was such a time. In no
cause was she more determined than in matters of
revenge.

'I believe there is madness in that Barton family,' she
murmured, her lips tight together.

Isobel de Vaux Banham had, as everyone knew, a fine
aristocratic background, but her family had been unfortunate enough to be on the losing side during the
English Civil War. Her earliest childhood memories
were from the time of Cromwell's Commonwealth,
which was what he called his personal dictatorship, and
she had seen her defeated Royalist family slowly stripped
of all its wealth and its estates. This was how she, who
should have grown up to be a grand lady with a retinue,
had her lands reduced to a small farm in Chapel Folding.
She ruled the farm as if it were her lost estate, but in
reality she had few servants, and consequently had
become more and more of a recluse, living in a world of
her own fantasy. Judge Nathan Mandeville, who had
once been her sweetheart and was now a very powerful
man, liked to indulge her in her dreams, and on the rare
occasions that he found time to visit her, she could feel

that she was somebody again. No-one in the neighbour-hood could laugh at her and her airs while he was there.

She knew the Bartons. They were farmers, way below her in social status, and a daughter of a Barton would be quite unsuitable as a match for her beloved nephew Peter Edmonton, whom she cared for like a son, having no children of her own. Worse still, the men of the Barton family were known to have been Roundheads, and during the Civil War they had supported Cromwell in his murderous insurrection. She was even convinced that a fair part of their wealth had been stolen directly from her own family, and that she could never forgive or forget. She knew that Peter had, in all probability, quite innocently fallen for a Barton, but it felt like a gross betrayal, and she could not prevent the bile from rising inside her. All her resentment about her reduced circum-stances was behind it.

When Cathy left school later that day, she found that the other children were talking together in groups, but not to her. This made her feel very uncomfortable. She took her little brother Mark with her and hurried up to the field where she had seen Ralph working earlier that morning. The countryside was lit up with patches of bright sun-light which pierced the clouds quite magically, but she was disappointed to discover that the field was only half ploughed, and Ralph was nowhere to be seen.

'Can we go home now?' said Mark, after he had watched his sister looking this way and that for some time. But Cathy had noticed that a group of village women had gathered at one corner of the field, and as she walked towards them, she could see that one of them was their mother, Ellen. Mark had now also spotted her and began to run towards her. When she saw them coming, partly in welcome, but also to keep them both away from the other women, she hurried forward and caught him.

'Come along,' she said.

'Where's Ralph?' asked Cathy before her mother had a chance to shepherd them away.

'Yon Ralph Gower saw som'ert that weren't right,' called out a dark-haired woman who had overheard her, 'not right at all!'

'Ralph is fine,' contradicted Ellen, as she led her children away. 'He had a bit of a shock earlier on, and had to go home, but he's alright. You'll see him in the morning.' Although her mother's words seemed quite definite and reassuring as usual, Cathy could not stop herself from looking back at the group of women, who were still chattering away, and who turned and looked repeatedly in their direction. Despite what she had said, Ellen Vespers had a worried expression on her face as they walked back to the farm. Cathy had never known it to be different. It was the sad countenance of a potential martyr, who had some curious premonition of the terrible series of events which were soon to overtake her. Of course, none of her doubts and fears would she ever communicate to her children. She gathered them under her wing like a mother hen, assuring them that all would be well.

'Do you remember young Peter, Mistress Banham's nephew?' said Ellen, adding, 'I'm sure you do. They say he has a sweetheart and has run away with her. We may even see him soon.' Rumours were circulating at the farm, from snatches of conversation overheard between Isobel and the Judge, and they were full of the details of Peter's clandestine romance. Ever the dreamer, Cathy was captivated by the idea of young lovers running away, for whatever reason, and she immediately wondered if one day she might run away with Ralph, although she knew there was no real purpose for them to do so. 'Elope', that was the word.

As soon as they arrived back at the farmhouse, a voice from upstairs called Ellen to her duties and she had to go.

'Where have you been?' cried Isobel sharply. 'I need you to prepare the spare room, and put a straw mattress in it, and get rid of the spiders.' Ellen knew that that dismal room in the attic was hardly ever used. She had convinced herself there were things moving about up there, and never liked to go there alone. All her fears had grown much worse now she had heard the story of Ralph's gruesome discovery. It felt as if the demon Ralph had found had woken all the ghosts in the village. She kept these fears from her children, though she wondered why she was suddenly being called upon to clean that particular room. She would need all her courage to do it, but she knew better than to ask the reason, or question her mistress in any way. Cathy and Mark looked at each other. Unaccountable and possibly exciting things were happening, ever since the Judge had arrived.

Peter Edmonton and his beloved Rosalind had, by chance, made their bid for freedom on the same inauspicious day that Ralph Gower had begun to plough in Tarrant's Field. A row between Rosalind and her red-faced father, in which he rashly told her that she must never see Peter again, had precipitated it.

Peter met her at dawn, in a little brick hut at the end of her garden, with his great horse tethered out of sight. Taking the shivering girl in his arms and roping her bags to the horse, he set off at some speed, bound for Chapel Folding, a day's journey away. Peter knew how much his aunt had always cared for him. She had looked after him no matter what, and although other people found her difficult, he had never encountered those difficulties. He was confident that she would welcome him and his new love with generosity. Rosalind, for her part, was full of amazement as to how events in her life were developing, and how fast it all had been, but she had made her decision, and was leaving her home and its walled garden behind her, probably for ever.

Later that same day, as twilight began to descend, Cathy was the first to see a horse approaching down the valley, with two people riding it. She sensed straight away who it might be and ran out to meet them. Peter saw her coming and called her name. As she finally caught up with them in the lane leading to the farmyard, the tired horse seemed to recognise its destination, and put on a little speed, which made it hard for her to keep up, but she did her best.

'Is it really true? You eloped?' she called out. 'Did you climb down a ladder in the moonlight?' Rosalind smiled at Cathy's enthusiasm, as she jumped up and down while she followed them, as if she meant to leap on the horse herself.

'No ladder,' said Peter.

'It was a little easier than that,' Rosalind added.

But it had been a long, uncomfortable journey even though Peter had sought to make Rosalind's ride as easy as possible. They had been in the saddle since dawn, and now both were exhausted.

'I want to elope someday,' said Cathy.

'Do you indeed?' said Peter with some amusement, as he descended from the horse. He then helped Rosalind down, while Cathy took over the task of soothing the tired animal and leading it to the stables. She stroked its big muzzle affectionately.

*

Looking out from her small, latticed window, Ellen Vespers had now become aware of the new figures in the yard, and she hurried out of her room, eager to bring the news to her mistress.

'Mister Peter is coming,' she said breathlessly, 'and with a young lady. Must be his intended.'

Isobel Banham feigned to show no interest at all.

'Farmer Barton's daughter,' she then said, distastefully.

'Isn't it wonderful?' said Ellen, losing none of her excitement. 'We shall have a new young mistress in the house!'

'I don't see the wonder of it, Ellen,' said Isobel, 'and she will not be staying.'

Rosalind was wandering round the yard, stretching her aching legs, and looking with great pleasure and interest at her new surroundings, as if her Peter had given her the beauty of them as a gift. She ran and gave him a big kiss.

'Am I fit to meet your aunt?' said Rosalind, looking hard in Peter's eyes. 'I pray she will like me.'

'To be sure she will,' said Peter. Rosalind was one of those vivacious people that it was impossible not to like. It was only her family who were being unreasonable, in seeking to prevent the match. She had an extremely expressive face which was always smiling or laughing or crying, and Cathy took to her immediately as if she were, despite the difference in their upbringing, her own big sister.

Peter knocked at the dark oak door of the farmhouse, surprised to find that it was already unlocked, and opened a little with his knocking. Rosalind, clutching her two small bags, looked at him nervously. He was tall, much taller than her, and she loved him dearly, though even in the half-light he did not look healthy or sturdy enough for farm work. He was out of his depth here. He was definitely a child of the town. He slowly pushed open the door, which gave on to an empty hall, dark and unwelcoming. Peter spoke as loud as he dared.

'Are you there, Aunt? I want you to meet Rosalind Barton.' There was no response, but voices could be heard murmuring from a room further in the house. He led an increasingly anxious Rosalind towards them. To make their presence felt, he was obliged to interrupt an ongoing conversation between his aunt and the Judge, but he did so with a smile.

'I said I might bring someone with me as a surprise, and here she is.'

Isobel behaved as if Rosalind were not there.

'Peter, it is a great inconvenience that you come at such a late hour. We were expecting you much earlier. The Judge was deeply hurt when you did not arrive to dine with him. He has done so much for you, and it is foolish to offend him so.'

Peter was taken aback. He had imagined that the hour of his arrival was a matter of no importance. It was surely the introduction of Rosalind that mattered. The Judge himself said nothing about his being late but looked at him severely. There was a long and embarrassing silence, until Rosalind plucked up the courage to give a short, prepared speech.

'It is an honour to meet you, Mistress Banham. Your home is most pleasantly situated.' Another silence. She held out her hand, which wasn't taken. Peter tried to gloss things over by pulling out a chair for Rosalind to sit on. She chose to remain standing, until invited by Isobel.

'We have had a troublesome day,' said Isobel, taking Peter aside so she could speak to him in private. Once out of earshot, she whispered to him severely, 'I hope that you are not expecting she should spend the night here.'

'Naturally I expect it. It is common courtesy,' said Peter, aloud, upset by his aunt's unusual behaviour. 'I am sorry if I have caused you inconvenience, but what possible harm is there if Rosalind spends the night here?'

'In your room?'

'I shall be very comfortable here, on the settle.'

'It is not right.'

'Dear Aunt, I have to tell you I intend to pay a visit to the Reverend Fallowfield tomorrow at first light, to request him to marry us. I am sure he will agree, then everything will be alright.'

Isobel Banham was speechless. The situation was far worse than she had thought. She gave a pleading glance in the direction of the Judge.

'Everything is not alright, young man. If you hope to

marry Miss Barton, it is most incorrect that she should spend the night under the same roof as her intended. Quite incorrect. The young lady should go home.'

'It is impossible, sir,' said Peter. The Judge was silent for a while, eyeing Rosalind up and down.

'I hope she is not expecting?'

'No, sir,' said Rosalind quickly. There was another pause.

'Good, then I believe we should all sit down and have a glass of wine,' he said. 'Nothing should be rushed in matters like this.'

'I thank you, my lord,' said Rosalind, with a brief curtsey before she sat.

Isobel had no choice but to accede to the Judge's request. After sharing a carafe of wine, he called for playing cards, and then suggested that they should lighten the atmosphere with a game. He made it very clear to Peter that he wanted no more talk of weddings. Time would tell.

The Judge and Isobel became natural partners, playing against Peter and Rosalind, and in game after game they had little competition. Rosalind had no knowledge of playing cards, which had been forbidden in her household, and could not tell a knave from a king. She constantly had to ask Peter to explain to her how to play each game. She tried to laugh off the situation with apologies for her incompetence, but Isobel and the Judge remained deadly serious. Although there was no money on the table, it appeared as if the stakes were high. After every game more wine was called for, and the unfortunate Rosalind began to suffer from attacks of drowsiness after her long day. Isobel longed to stamp on her pretty little foot under the table, if only to hear her squeal.

'Your elders triumph,' said the Judge.

'It does not appear that Miss Barton is the perfect partner for you, Peter,' said Isobel, pointedly. 'No doubt in other respects she will do better?'

Unable to take any more, Rosalind rose from her seat.

'I hope you will all excuse me if I retire.'

The Judge nodded and gathered up the cards. Peter also rose. Rosalind waited to be guided to her bedroom. Isobel said nothing.

'You still haven't decided where my betrothed shall sleep,' protested Peter.

'Well, the Judge will certainly be passing the night here, and he shall have your room, Peter.'

'But in that case, where can Rosalind sleep?'

'She shall have the spare room.'

'The attic room? No-one sleeps there.'

Peter looked to the Judge for support, but he now sensed that Isobel and the Judge were in league.

'Ellen,' called out Isobel, imperiously, 'will you be so kind as to conduct Miss Barton to the spare room.' Ellen soon appeared, holding a candle, almost as if she had been listening at the door.

46

'It hasn't been inhabited these five years,' said Peter. 'The room is filthy.'

'Tush, it is a charming room,' returned Isobel. 'Ellen has prepared it.'

Rosalind was led out by Ellen, and the Judge poured Peter another glass of wine, leaning across as if he wished to talk to him in confidence. Peter hesitated, but then got to his feet, unnerved by the situation. He was trying to make sense of what was going on, and might have welcomed some explanation from the Judge, but he was too concerned about Rosalind. Much to the obvious disapproval of his aunt, he picked up Rosalind's bags and followed her and Ellen upstairs.

As she led Rosalind up to the attic, Ellen tried to make an apology for the strange behaviour of her mistress.

'You must understand, miss, it has been a most unusual day. Some sort of animal was seen in the fields, and the whole village has been talking ever since.'

'An animal?'

'Can't say what it was, miss, but Mistress Banham was most upset by it, I could see. She's not her normal self, you understand. Not at all.'

Inwardly Rosalind hoped that this was right, as she had been quite unprepared for Isobel's hostility.

Ellen smiled at her reassuringly as they climbed the winding stairs. The house was much taller than it appeared from outside, and in the half-light the staircase seemed to curve endlessly before they reached the door of the spare room. Rosalind grew more and more nervous but was relieved to see Peter following them.

'Good night, miss,' said Ellen, as she opened the door. 'Things will be better in the morning, I'm sure.' And she discreetly withdrew, allowing the two lovers a few private moments together.

Peter found it hard to hide his disgust at the room where Rosalind was being forced to sleep. It was less a bedroom than a storeroom, and it only had one tiny window. The bed was just a mattress on the floor, with a little wooden table, a taper and a tinder box beside it. Not only was the low ceiling sloping, but the floor also sloped downwards, as was often the case in old houses, and the effect was very disorientating, like a ship at sea.

'It is only for tonight,' he said.

'Oh, Peter, do I have to sleep here? Why does your aunt dislike me so much?'

'Be patient,' he replied, and lowering his voice he added, 'and I promise I'll come to you at eleven o'clock, when my aunt and the Judge are both asleep.' His conspiratorial smile quickly turned Rosalind's mood from fear to excitement, as they now had an assignation and a secret. Perhaps the mad situation they were in would soon improve.

'And all will be well tomorrow when I see the priest,' Peter added, taking her in his arms.

'I do love you!' she murmured.

But Peter could not stay long. Ellen was still waiting, and he was expected downstairs.

'Better you go now,' said Rosalind. 'Your aunt . . .'

'Eleven, then,' Peter repeated, and was gone.

Left alone, Rosalind took stock of the place where she had to sleep. The room was stacked with unwanted furniture and family heirlooms, covered in dust sheets; chests, sideboards, even something huge and lumbering that looked like a broken throne. It was as if a living tableau had been frozen and suddenly covered. She decided that it was better not to lift any of the sheets, as she was afraid that some of the chairs might prove to be occupied.

Taking off her heavy travelling clothes, she lay on the bed and waited. The wait was a long one. Her taper burnt down until it smouldered and went out. Then, as she struggled to keep herself awake, she began to hear noises. It seemed that something was moving about behind the furniture, or underneath the floor. She had once visited a house overrun with rats, and she remembered what strength they had, how they could lift whole floorboards to get where they wanted. The thought did not cheer her much, and it was not long before the room was peopled with her fears, and still no sign of Peter. She began to get the shakes. She could feel the hairs creeping up her arms, and she shivered. An animal, Ellen had said. What kind of animal? All the nightmares of her childhood were beginning to revisit her.

Peter tried to talk directly to his aunt and tell her that Rosalind needed to be treated gently. She was fragile, with little experience of the world, and had taken a great risk by running away from her overbearing Puritan family for his sake. But Isobel's eyes had glazed over completely, and it was impossible to speak to her. The Judge, who was not for sleeping, raised his glass in a toast.

'To his Catholic Majesty, King James the Third. God bless him and keep him in exile!'

With that he drained his wine to the dregs and threw the empty glass into the fireplace. Isobel jerked at this, like a frightened bird, but it was the effect on Peter that most interested him. The toast was, of course, treasonous. But Nathan Mandeville knew that Rosalind Barton's family were deeply committed Protestants. Would Peter now support them for Rosalind's sake, against the boy king James, the exiled king of the defeated Catholics? Peter sat there silently, full of embarrassment, hoping that the whole dreadful evening would soon end.

Then suddenly, without a word, Isobel rose from her seat and floated out of the room. The Judge sat there glumly in drunken solemnity.

'You've made a big mistake, my boy,' he said at last when she had gone. 'You don't realise what you've done. Your aunt feels betrayed.' He gave no explanation as to how Peter had betrayed his aunt, and Peter could think of nothing to say in his own defence. It was all too incomprehensible. He tried to get to his feet, but the Judge pulled him back.

'You should know that there is madness in the Barton family,' he said, 'and this very much worries your aunt. Old Marjorie Barton quite suddenly became completely lunatic and boiled her husband in the bath.' Peter had heard some such story, but it had nothing to do with Rosalind.

'That was a long time ago, and I don't even believe it was true,' he said. The Judge shrugged his shoulders and withheld his opinion.

'All the same, you should be circumspect with a family of the wrong religion,' he went on. Peter had never thought that the Judge had any particular interest in religion. He was a practical man and a believer in science, a friend of Thomas Savery, the inventor of the steam pump. Although he was technically, as Peter had just learnt, a Jacobite, he had never discussed politics or religion before, only the power of the law. He began to engage Peter in a long, rambling and drunken conversation about the evils of the Bartons and the unbelievers, and then about bad women in general, the purpose of which seemed to be to prevent him from going to bed. It was as if he knew Peter had plans and was determined to thwart them.

'Beware the wiles of women,' he said, and embarked on a long lecture, in which he confessed that as a young man he had once become captivated by Peter's aunt.

Eleven o'clock was soon past, and the loud brass clock with its thin metal face was ticking beyond midnight.

Then the Judge heard something which made him pause, and suddenly, without a word, he snatched the candlestick from the table, leaving Peter with only the dying light of the fire, and set off for bed. Peter was painfully aware how long it had been since Rosalind had gone to her room – half the night, it seemed. In case the Judge returned, he made much pretence of preparing himself a bed on the settle with bedclothes left him by Ellen, and then he waited for a short while until he was completely sure there was not a sound from the Judge or his aunt. Finally, he left the room and began to creep up the dark wood staircase towards the attic.

Rosalind, who had by then fallen asleep, was woken by a click of the latch. At first, she shuddered, then she smiled. In the darkness she could see that the door had opened, just a little.

'Peter?' she whispered, but there was no further movement. The door remained slightly ajar. She moved down to the end of the bed.

'Peter, is that you?' Silence. Still no movement. Why was he not coming in?

Suddenly, a huge shadowy creature came through the door and scuttled round the room, moving almost too fast for her eyes to follow it. For a while it disappeared behind the sheeted furniture, and then it leapt into the bed with her.

Peter was halfway up the stairs when the screaming began. It was terrible and continuous. With no further need for secrecy, he ran up to Rosalind's door as fast as he could, but the door wouldn't open. It was as if a heavy piece of furniture had been moved against it, and still the screaming went on. There was soon a thundering on the stairs behind him, and the Judge, woken by all the noise, was at his side. Between the two of them they finally succeeded in pushing the door open. The screaming by then had stopped, and he could see Rosalind in her nightdress, curled up in a ball on the far side of the room, whimpering. He wanted to run across to her, but the Judge, who was a strong man, held him back, looking around to be sure there was no other presence in the room with her. Isobel now came up behind them. Peter turned towards her just as she reached them, and she staggered back a step.

'What is going on?' she demanded. 'You almost knocked me down. What was all that noise?'

'Rosalind . . .' Peter began.

'What have you been doing, Peter? What have you been doing?' She pushed past both Peter and the Judge, glaring at Peter as if he had caused all the trouble, and entered the room herself. Peter wanted to follow her, but the Judge firmly pulled him away.

'Rosalind!' Peter called again, and struggled with the Judge, who eventually resorted to hitting him full in the face, as he might a hysteric.

'Stand back!'

They waited a few steps down, watching intently while Isobel went to reason with Rosalind, who was still cowering and whimpering in the corner.

'You vile little Barton!' snorted Isobel, beating her repeatedly. 'You little vixen; you've made yourself bleed deliberately.' But then she gave a shriek and came running out of the room and down the stairs, with blood streaming down her own face.

'She scratched me,' she cried. 'The little devil scratched me!'

'Ellen!' called the Judge. 'Peter, you go and look after your poor aunt!' But Peter did not want to look after her. She could look after herself, he thought; besides, Rosalind had now sprung to her feet, and appeared at the door. She stood there quietly, with a strange smile on her face. It was apparent to Peter that she neither saw nor recognised him. The Judge whispered to Peter, 'She is a danger to herself and to others. I have been to Bedlam, and I know those empty eyes.'

'Bedlam?' said Peter. Rosalind began to moan.

'Peter, you must go. Your presence at this time will only disturb her.' The Judge said this with such authority that Peter felt obliged to obey his advice and back away. Ellen and another servant then appeared at the foot of the stairs. Ellen was very alarmed to see her mistress bleeding now quite badly, and she led her into the kitchen to look for unguents, and bandages for her wounds. The Judge slowly edged towards Rosalind, who stood quietly, staring into space, with blood dripping from her nightgown, then turned away from him fearfully and went back into the room. He took advantage of the moment and closed the door, stationing himself in front of it to prevent her from leaving.

'Nobody is to go in there until help is sent for,' he called to the whole household. 'Her condition is dangerous.'

Peter protested, 'Rosalind is not mad.'

'She is beyond our reach. Your aunt is badly wounded. Judge yourself fortunate, young man. She would never have been a fit wife for you.'

He then called out again, 'I want nails and some wood! And send for a doctor to treat Mistress Banham!'

Ralph arrived at the farm in the early morning as the mists were rising. He was anxious to see Cathy again, to tell her what had happened on the previous day, and why he had left off ploughing. He was greeted by the scene of a disaster. A groom from the stables, who was a friend of his, came up to him as soon as he arrived, and begged for his help. His mistress had suffered some terrible wounds on her face. The door to the attic room needed to be mended and nailed shut, but none of the servants dared to go near it.

'Why?' said Ralph.

'Do not ask,' was the reply.

As he followed the terrified groom upstairs, Ralph found that far from being regarded as a ploughman who ran away from his work, he was now regarded as a hero who had looked the devil in the face without flinching, and the servants believed that, for some reason, he was the only person strong enough to bar up the spare-room door.

He passed by Peter Edmonton, whom he recognised at once, and would have bid him good day, but he was sitting at the big table with his head in his hands, defeated and weeping, and Ralph did not like to disturb him. Altogether, he did not always understand the ways of his masters. Some tragedy had occurred, it seemed, but only they knew what it was.

What greeted him at the top of the stairs deeply shocked him. Planks of wood were lying about with nails still in them. One piece of wood remained, nailed loosely across the door, which had been attacked from inside and broken. In places it had burst completely open with spikes of smashed wood sticking out, as if some wild animal had charged it from within. All the same, Ralph was not to be daunted. He set about reinforcing the door, and was making a good job of it, when, having stopped hammering for a moment, he heard a sobbing.

'There's som'on in there!' he called out.

'To be sure there is! For God's sake bar the door!' the groom called from below.

'A woman,' said Ralph, but even as he spoke, the woman's sobs turned into a deep growl.

'You don't want to know,' said the groom. 'Finish your work and come you down.'

Deeply alarmed, Ralph did as he was told. Servants were not supposed to ask questions.

The local doctor, Isaiah Grubb, had always been a regular visitor at Isobel Banham's farm, as she was subject to a variety of imaginary illnesses caused by 'weak nerves'. He came with a half-empty bag, clutching his little quarto edition of Nicholas Culpeper's *Herbal*, which he didn't expect to use. Whatever the symptoms, Isobel's underlying illness was always the same, loneliness, and that could easily be cured with a friendly chat and a couple of drinks. On this day, however, things were different. He could already see it on Ellen's face as she greeted him. Even the old Judge who was staying at the farmhouse seemed very concerned about Isobel's health.

The doctor found her lying in bed, propped up on pillows, with her face completely swathed in bandages which were tinged with patches of blood. She appeared to have been attacked. He looked with some slight suspicion at the little caged songbird next to the bed, but he very soon saw it was far worse than that. She was feverish, and barely able to recognise him. As he tried to undo the bandages, she turned her head from side to side, making his task nearly impossible. Also there was an infernal hammering coming from above that seemed to frighten her.

When he had unwrapped the bandages, he discovered three deep cuts right across her face, which were very hard to explain. It looked as if they had been caused by an encounter with a wild animal, but what? A wild cat or a lynx? If it were a bird, it could have been nothing less than a giant eagle. He was completely out of his depth. Culpeper could not help him here. Ellen watched him clean the cuts, but offered no explanation for them.

Then Isobel began to recover her senses. She looked at the doctor with alarm.

'What happened to me?'

He put a consoling hand on her wrist, feeling her pulse at the same time. It was very fast.

'You appear to have some distemper as yet unknown to me,' he said. 'I can open a vein and the humour may perhaps pass out.'

He told her there had been more and more strange cases recently, and he feared a plague. He didn't say what these cases were, and as his knowledge was rather limited, all but the most straightforward illnesses were often 'strange' to him. However, on the previous day he had visited an old woman, one of the gossips at the edge of the field, who also had a fever, and a curious furry rash on her arm. The doctor found such things fascinating. Isobel, on the other hand, was becoming more and more alarmed and confused.

'Have you some eau de vie?' he asked Ellen. Ellen dutifully disappeared to hunt for it and returned a little later with a bottle of brandy and a glass, but by the time she did so Isobel had subsided into sleep again. The doctor listened to her breathing. She seemed quite rested now, and he felt there was really nothing more he could do, so he drank the brandy himself, admonished Ellen to take good care of her mistress, and left.

Peter had also been deeply disturbed by Ralph's hammering, not least because he was not sure if some of the noises he heard came from Rosalind herself as she banged on the door, begging to be released. It was horrible. He had risen from the table and paced around anxiously, but still could not bring himself to go up the stairs. In any case the servants had been given firm instructions not to allow him to do so. Ralph came down soon after, his face very solemn, but the two men did not speak. Ralph was pleased to be out of the farmhouse and in the fresh air.

Later that afternoon the men from the bedlam arrived. Peter wanted to talk to them, but the Judge told him firmly that they knew what they were doing and would not harm the girl. They undid all of Ralph's good work with crowbars and removed the patient from the attic room. Rosalind came quietly, subdued and obedient. Although they were quite prepared to use force, they did not need to do so. All the same, for safety's sake, they put a firm leather belt around her.

Peter watched as they led her downstairs, and as she descended, she smiled at him. He smiled back encouragingly, and began to think that surely she might soon recover, but then her smile developed into a grin, addressed not to him but to the entire world. And then he saw that her hand, which protruded from her night-dress as she grasped the bannister, was not a human hand at all, but the claws of an animal. A sudden sickness welled up inside him and he had to turn away. That was the last he saw of her. When he gathered the courage to look up again, she had gone.

The Judge sat him down later with a flagon of strong ale, and told him he must be a man and accept that life does not always deal good cards. Those claws which he saw were not real, he told him, any more than Ralph's half-dead monster had been. They were an illusion caused by his disturbed state. Nobody else had seen them. The men from the bedlam mentioned no such thing, and he himself had seen nothing unusual. Such visions might be expected from a peasant like Ralph, but not from someone of Peter's standing. He must put them out of his mind.

'But . . .' Peter began, although seeing the Judge frown-ing grimly, he soon changed tack, 'Rosalind has shown no signs of any mental disorder in all of her life. She was so happy before she came here. This must just be a fit or a frenzy that will soon pass. Don't you agree?'

The Judge sighed.

'Perhaps she couldn't take the shock of the break with her family,' he said. 'She had the appearance of someone who led a very sheltered life, too sheltered. But one has to be realistic. I have in my time seen a number of people taken off to Bedlam. I have never seen anyone return.'

That night Isobel Banham had a dream. Recently she had been troubled by similar dreams, but this was much stronger and more vivid. From the heart of the woodland which covered the hills across from her farm there came an eerie bellowing, as of a beast in pain. The little bird at her bedside was in panic at the sound, fluttering against the wicker bars of its cage.

All the time it felt as if a shadow in the forest was growing, forming itself piece by piece out of the darkness, and as it did so, its grim cries became more and more human, and she could feel that it was calling her. All at once she was outside the farmhouse, barefoot on the grass, dressed in nothing but a nightgown, and she was a young girl again. In the cold night air, she felt exactly as she had done when she was twenty, a feeling of excitement that she had lost completely with the years. She was playing a part in a dark but beautiful fairy tale. She could hear music and dancing, which took her back to the time when she first discovered the joy of it, when Cromwell had gone and the deliciously wicked King Charles the Second was on the throne. But this music was different, and the dances were not the gavottes and galliards she had known in her youth. This music was fired by a more insistent and distinctly pagan rhythm, which came as if from beneath the ground. The beast was calling her. She walked across Tarrant's half-ploughed field and into the woods, enveloped by the shade of the trees. She knew he would be there, waiting for her. He would take her in his warm, dark arms, while from his jaws came the harsh metallic smell of blood, dripping from the kill. She shook with a mixture of terror and ecstasy such as she had rarely felt in her life before. Even before she reached him, she could feel his presence, and his claws carving their way down her back. 'You are mine,' he said. 'You have my skin.'

Chapter Four

The Claw

After Ralph Gower had left off ploughing Tarrant's Field, and the stories about his discovery there had begun to spread, nobody from the village would dream of going near the place; nobody, that is, except for the children. Ignoring the good advice of their elders, they were out there at first light, fearlessly hunting for bones and eyeballs or any ghoulish object which could relate to what Ralph Gower was supposed to have seen, and which they, in their innocence, hoped they might easily find. Their searches were mostly fruitless, but they did not give up, until every so often, one of them could claim to have discovered something. It was then examined excitedly by everyone until it was found to be just an oddly shaped stone, an animal bone, or a snail shell, and so tossed away. All the same, with each new find, they enjoyed frightening each other with the thought of what it might be.

Unaware of what had been happening in her household, and kept well in the dark by her mother, Cathy Vespers was still full of the excitement caused by the rumour that there was to be a wedding at the farm. Peter was to visit the Reverend Fallowfield this very morning, and he and Rosalind were to get married. Cathy went looking for Mark to tell him, but discovered that, in disobedience to their mother, he had gone to join the children hunting for trophies in Tarrant's Field. She hurried up there herself to fetch him back, but he wouldn't come. Her school friends, Angel Blake and Winsome Rogers, were there too, and Tim Parsons was with them, and a few others. Angel tried to persuade Cathy to join them, but she stood aloof.

'You look. I don't want to,' she said.

'Cathy's afeard!' Angel said to Mark, who laughed.

'I bain't,' said Cathy, 'but Mark should come home. There's to be a wedding at the farm.'

'A wedding?' said Angel.

'Ma said we weren't to talk of weddings,' said Mark, and continued hunting. Cathy had no choice but to join him, searching the ground fruitlessly for a while before she let through another thought, which had been troubling her, although she had told no-one.

'I heard screams last night,' she said.

'You dreamed 'em, you mean,' said Mark.

But at the least mention of screams, Tim and Winsome wanted to hear more. Was it to do with the beast? Was he even now roaming through the village?

'Angel, did you hear?' called Tim. 'Cathy heard someone screaming in Mistress Banham's farm last night.'

But Angel wasn't listening. She had gone off on her own and had spotted something very exciting. It was possibly the treasure she had hoped for. She leapt across a raised furrow and pounced on it. She grew more and more delighted by her new discovery, but straight away she hid it. She wasn't about to tell anyone what it was.

'Let's see!' cried the others, but Angel didn't want them to see. Unlike the other children, who proudly showed off their little trophies, Angel hid hers in the folds of her skirt and ran away. Mark ran after her.

'Give it us!' he called out. 'I want to see.'

Suddenly Angel rounded on him, giving him an unexpectedly fierce look, which stopped him in his tracks.

'Thou must do a forfeit,' she said, with a peculiar malice in her voice. What she meant by this no-one knew, but she soon ran off again, with Mark and Cathy in pursuit.

When she thought no-one was looking, Angel hid her discovery in a little bag. She would tell nobody what it was until the time was ripe, but this prompted some of the boys to say that she was lying and had not found anything at all. Angel treated this with contempt, telling them they would soon learn. Despite or because of her secretiveness, the interest among the other children began to grow, and Angel, with her hidden treasure, became the acknowledged leader of the scavengers. Mark boasted to the others that he had seen it when she slipped it in her bag, and that it was a finger or a claw. Angel did not confirm or deny this. She simply told them that it had special powers.

When Ralph met Cathy later, he was shocked to find she had been up on Tarrant's Field and warned her strongly against it. He also had to disillusion her about there being any prospect of a wedding. Something terrible had happened, and Peter Edmonton was a broken man. He had himself seen Peter looking miserable and desolate, not at all how a prospective bridegroom ought to be. He did not say more, because he felt it was his duty to protect Cathy from too much speculation and rumour, and – as he kept telling himself – it was not his role as a servant to enquire into the affairs of his masters, or their sorrows. Her mother, Ellen, was of the same opinion and concentrated only on ensuring the recovery of her mistress from her unexplained illness.

Although she was still plagued by nightmares, Isobel Banham's health did begin to improve, and she left her bed for short walks. Her wounds were healing, leaving only a small rash which came from a scratch on her left shoulder. She had not mentioned this to the doctor, as it did not hurt her, and it was surrounded by an increasing growth of body hair, a curious development which she decided to keep private, as it was embarrassing to a lady of standing to be thought of as growing hair like an animal.

Despite the disappearance of Rosalind from the scene, Isobel's coldness towards her nephew Peter did not decrease. She still felt that he had betrayed her, and although she was prepared to tolerate his presence in her house for a little while longer, that was all she was prepared to do, and he was not ever to mention the name of Barton.

Peter remained deeply despondent. His whole world had collapsed, and it seemed that there was nothing he could do to rebuild it. The Judge had warned him that if he attempted to visit Rosalind in the madhouse, he would not be admitted. It was their policy that new patients must be locked away and not disturbed. Dark, despairing thoughts of suicide began to enter his mind. He could not live without her.

'It's a sorry time for us all,' said Ellen to Dr Grubb, who had called again to see his patient, carrying a large book under his arm. 'And the young master's heart is quite broke.'

'Ellen!' called Isobel from her room.

'Just you lie quiet, my lady,' Ellen replied. 'The doctor tells me you need rest. I'll fetch you a hot milk and be with you straight away.'

'Ellen!' Isobel called again, plaintively.

Dr Grubb went to show the Judge the old book which

he had found. It was a book of devils, a witch-hunter's guide, and contained depictions of satanic figures, witches' familiars, and the like. He opened it in front of the Judge for him to see.

'There,' he said, pointing at one of the devils. 'Is that not exactly like him?'

'Who?' said the Judge.

'The creature Ralph Gower discovered, what he saw.'

'So, you believe in that nonsense, do you?' grumbled the Judge. It was not the reaction that Dr Grubb had hoped for.

'Could it not be that what we have here is a case of demonic possession?' he asked. 'Or witchcraft?'

'Good God, Doctor,' said the Judge, 'as a man of science, do you expect to restore Miss Barton from the bedlam and dear Isobel from the vapours by conjuring with monkeys?' He indicated the contorted little figures and crude woodcuts in the book.

'No, but surely,' stammered the doctor, 'all kinds of insane fancies are said to be created around images such as these . . .'

'Learning and superstition make poor companions,' said the Judge, firmly shutting the book. 'You should think twice before you start spreading stories of witchcraft, or people will imagine you are a warlock yourself.'

This felt rather like a threat. The doctor rose to his feet with his book held firmly under his arm, determined now to keep his thoughts private.

'I do not have anything against your curious and unusual remedies, you understand,' said the Judge, in a more genial tone. 'There was a time when I thought to follow your profession myself, but finally the law took my fancy. You have power over men's bodies, but I have power over their lives.'

In the kitchen Ellen took a ladle of milk from a pitcher and warmed it over the fire. Outside, on the road, she could hear the sound of children singing and chanting to the beat of a drum. She wondered what they were doing, as it seemed very unusual, even a little disturbing. Carefully she added to the warm milk a little of Dr Grubb's panacea, his eau de vie, which she thought would help her mistress to sleep. She then carried it up to Isobel's room. When she arrived, the room was so silent that she thought her mistress must have fallen asleep, and was at first afraid to disturb her, but then she sensed that something was very wrong. She noticed that the bird cage was open, and the songbird had gone. There was a heap of twisted bedclothes on the bed, but no Isobel. She was not in the closet, nor anywhere in the suite of rooms which she normally occupied.

'Mistress Banham, where art thou?' she called out. 'Has anyone seen the lady of the house?'

Nobody had seen her, nor had any idea that she had gone from her room. It seemed as if she had vanished into thin air. The Judge knew nothing of her whereabouts, but was worried, and his growing concern began to infect everybody else. Isobel had been calling for Ellen just before she disappeared. Had she seen something? Had she needed help? Ellen felt guilty that she had not reached her sooner. The children's chanting had now stopped, she noticed, and the house felt very quiet and empty.

Peter asked if it were not possible that his aunt had simply gone to visit someone in the village, but Ellen was adamant that she was still too ill to go anywhere. Even in normal times she rarely left her home to go visiting. All the same, the Judge ordered enquiries to be made from house to house.

He then walked out into the yard and looked around at the woods, as if he might somehow be able to guess where she had gone just by scanning the pathways and gaps in the trees. He could see that the sky was darkening, and it was coming on to rain. What could she be doing out there?

'Fetch the local magistrate,' he called to a servant. 'It is his job to keep order here.' He might have added that he was almost certain that the magistrate was well acquainted with Isobel Banham, was indeed a friend of hers, and would be best equipped to find her.

Squire Middleton showed great disdain at being disturbed by Isobel's servant and being ordered to attend to a problem which would probably solve itself. She would be found somewhere, safe and sound. She was not a fool. However, on discovering that the message had come from Isobel's influential friend, Judge Mandeville, his attitude changed completely. Although he could be a bully towards those who were below him, when it came to men of great importance like a High Court judge from London, he could not be more subservient. He had been aching for an invitation to meet the man. Despite the rain, he immediately made his way in person to Isobel Banham's farm.

'I shall put all my men at your disposal,' he said to the Judge. 'No blade of grass shall remain unturned, and if she be hiding anywhere, or dead in a ditch, we will find her.' His bustling mixture of enthusiasm and insensitivity met with a chilly response from the Judge.

'Of course you will find her, Squire,' he said, with a look which suggested there might be consequences if he failed. 'That is your duty, is it not?'

Ralph was sent for, and together with a group of men from Squire Middleton's estate, he set off across the fields and into the rain, looking for a sixty-year-old woman in her nightclothes who had wandered off for no known reason. Hours passed and no word came back. Meanwhile, the rainstorm only worsened.

Faced with the loss of his beloved and now the sudden disappearance of his aunt, Peter sat silently, buried deep in his own thoughts, listening to the waves of rainwater on the windows.

'There's evil in this house,' he whispered.

'You must cleanse your mind of such fantasies,' said

the Judge with some annoyance. The Squire also looked for a long while at Peter, but expressions of sympathy were not really his strong suit. Instead, he addressed himself to the Judge.

'Will you sup with me tonight, my lord?' he said. 'It is only humble fare, but the finest in the shire.'

'Thank you, Squire,' replied the Judge. 'I remain here tonight. The lady was a dear friend of mine.'

'Naturally,' said the Squire, humbled and not a little disappointed.

It was a long while before the sound of men and horses could be heard again in the yard. The search party had at last returned. Squire Middleton went out to meet them. Peter could see him gesticulating and waving his stick at them through the window. The men were soaked through, muddy and exhausted, but their search had met with no success. The Squire, who had hoped to impress the Judge with his efficiency, now had to admit that his men had failed, and that made him very angry. He sent them on their way. No success meant no reward.

'They lost the scent completely, my lord,' he said as he returned. 'My hounds would have done better! To have wandered so far in this weather, she must have the constitution of an ox!'

'She was a sick woman,' said the Judge.

'Indeed, my lord, as you say, she was a sick woman.' The Squire then came up with his own thoughts on the matter.

'I must confess I fear there is something very strange afoot. Did you hear what Gower turned up with his plough?'

'Justice Middleton,' said the Judge gruffly, 'I myself examined those furrows. There was nothing.'

'Yes, of course, there was nothing,' the Squire replied, careful not to give further offence. Since there was nothing to be found and nothing more he could do, he decided to take his leave.

'Damnable business, Mr Edmonton, eh?' he said to the silent Peter as he passed. 'Fear nothing. At first light the hunt goes on!'

The door closed, the latch fell, leaving Peter and the Judge alone in the farmhouse. Each had their own sadness, but they could communicate little of it to the other. There was a dark emptiness in the silent house, and the rain-filled woods around it felt ever more sinister and threatening. There were goblins out there.

The Judge took a grim view of the situation. After so long in such a storm it did not now seem likely that a sick Isobel would be found alive, and Rosalind was also as good as dead to the world. He poured for himself and Peter a stiff drink. The two men watched in silence as the embers lay dying in the fire, snaking their way among the ashes.

Peter abruptly announced his intention to sleep in the spare room, where Rosalind had slept on the night of the disaster. In his rather drunken state, he hoped that if something in that room had carried her off, he might find out what it was, and fight with it. It might destroy him in the end, but that hardly mattered. His only thought was to be as close to her, or her memory, as he could. The Judge was surprised by his strange decision, but his reaction was, *Why not let him? Sometimes a tough cure is the best one.*

He poured himself another large whisky and gave one more to Peter for the night.

'It is getting late,' he said. 'You had better go to your room, young man, and I will go to mine. Where's Ellen? I need a candle.'

Peter watched him disappear in the direction of the kitchen. He then picked up the old oil lamp from beside the fireplace. It was still thundering outside, as the dying rainstorm continued on its slow path into the far distance. Peter climbed the stairs past his aunt's empty room, and muttered a silent 'good night' outside her door, as if she were still there.

As he crept further up the stairs, Peter could hazily imagine that Rosalind was still waiting for him at the top. In the flickering darkness he could even see her shadow beginning to open her door as if she were preparing to look out. As he came closer, she vanished, and he could see that the door was unwelcoming, and that it was battered and full of nails. He lightly touched the nails and could almost hear, in the very far distance, the screams and commotion of that dreadful night. The door staggered open. The bed was still unmade. Neither Ellen nor anyone else had visited that room since Rosalind left it. A little posy of wildflowers which she had collected on their long, hopeful journey was still lying on the bedside table and beginning to wilt. He set the oil lamp next to it. The lamp flustered at the mercy of the draughts, which followed the dying rain.

As he lay on the bed and toyed with the flowers, he could almost smell Rosalind lying there beside him. He remembered how she would yelp and laugh on the horse behind him when he spurred it into a canter. The memory was so real and so recent, but now he was in grim silence, and the dark, sheeted furniture seemed to watch him solemnly from around the room. In the distance below a door slammed. He presumed the Judge had gone to bed.

Peter discovered, not far from his bedside, a small case of clothes which had been overlooked when Rosalind had been taken away. A deep pain passed through him when he realised that these were wedding clothes which she had never shown him. He pulled them into the bed next to him, laying the posy on them. He then clutched at the clothes, drawing them to him as if they had been the body of their owner, and curled up with them on the bed.

Sleep was near to taking hold of him when he heard a scuffling, scratching noise beneath the floorboards. He opened his eyes wide, reaching out with his hand to turn up the oil lamp, but his movement was clumsy, and he sent the lamp crashing to the floor, spilling oil in all directions. He was only just able to prevent it from catching fire, although a low bluish flame hovered above it for a little while before it went out and plunged everything in darkness. He sat up in the bed, slowly adjusting his eyes to the moonlight which filtered through small gaps in the roof. He then heard another scuffling, similar to that he had heard before, but this time it was followed by a stifled squeal. He located the floorboard from which it came. As he pressed this board, it creaked and showed itself to be quite loose. Carefully inserting his fingers around the end, he prised it up with all his strength until it gave way, leaving a dark hole. He carefully felt inside this hole, and pulled out the body of a dead rat, covered with dust and fresh blood, and laid it on the floor. This should have been enough for him, but he was drunk and fearless and expected there was more. He felt around beneath the adjacent floorboards to see what he could find. It seemed to be only an empty space, and he was about to replace the floorboard when his arm was grabbed tight with a violent jerk. As he tried to pull it away, he could feel his hand clasped by another hand, a hand that had claws for fingers. He was only aware of this for a moment before his own hand slipped from the claws, and he took it out, sore and bleeding. He tried to get to his feet, but the room swam around him, and he came to the hazy conclusion that he must be dreaming.

In his dream, he backed away to the door, which would not open, as if the latch were caught. He opened his mouth to call for help, but no sound would come out. He looked at the gaping hole in the floor as if he expected something to leap out of it. Carefully, with his foot, he pushed the loose floorboard until it fell again into place. He then dragged a large, heavy piece of sheeted furniture over it, which caught it just as it was beginning to rise up again. He began to rummage among all the junk in the room until he could find something with which to protect himself, in case he were attacked. He happened upon a large old knife, which looked badly rusted, although when he tested the blade it seemed dangerously sharp in places, where it had not been eaten away. He looked around, but he did not have any immediate need for the knife as there was now no evidence of his unseen enemy, so he laid it on the bedside table within reach. He then collapsed back on the bed, listening to the movement of insects in the woodwork, and ready to grab the knife in an instant, until a deeper sleep fell upon him and he could move no more.

In the early hours, a group of unknown women in white shrouds were seen wandering through the village and disappearing into the woods near old Ned Carter's hovel. Accounts of this apparition varied but it became the subject of a great deal of gossip later in the day. It was thought that one of them was Isobel Banham, but no-one could be sure. The mists clung low over

Tarrant's Field and lost themselves like rumours among the trees.

When the first cock began to crow, Peter woke in fear, sensing the movement of something soft and sinister that was touching the side of his face. It was gentle and furry, but it did not belong to any of the clothes he had taken to bed with him. In his dreams it had been human hair, but when he woke it became something quite other. Its sharp talons were around his neck, already choking him, and its oily hair, more like that of a shaggy goat, seemed to belong to a being that was bigger and more powerful than he was. With his left hand he scrambled for the knife, and almost dropped it in the effort of getting a hold of it quickly. He slashed it across the arm of the animal that was strangling him, but it did not back off, only tightened its grip. He cut it again and again with the knife. The pain was excruciating. Blood gushed from the wound he made, but still the claws tightened, and he knew he was fighting for his life. He cut and cut it to the bone and gristle, until he had completely severed the hand from the arm. Only then did it release its grasp as the blood spurted and spread like a sea over the sheets. With that, he passed out.

The Judge, who had been woken by noises from above, burst into the room and discovered Peter with his hand completely severed at the wrist. Ellen was not far behind, but he motioned her back, fearing that she might not be able to take the shock.

'Water, Ellen, and bandages,' yelled the Judge. 'Send for the doctor! We have to stop the blood.' He tore the sheeting into strips to make a tourniquet. With this the blood was stopped from spurting. Ellen ran to fetch a bowl of water to clean the wound, calling out all the time:

'Ralph! Ralph, where are you? Fetch the doctor. Mister Peter's hurt himself bad!' Her voice echoed through the house and trailed away. Ralph, who was outside, working in the yard, called back, and then began running for the doctor.

The Judge washed Peter's shattered arm, and the curious wounds on his neck. Why would he do such a thing? The knife he had used was still in his left hand. It was terrifying, what the human mind would drive itself to do out of fear. He now allowed a greater credibility to Ralph's disturbing apparition, but at the same time was more determined than ever to rid the world of such dreadful illusions.

When Dr Grubb arrived, Peter was still unconscious in the attic room. The doctor told the Judge and Ellen that they had done exactly what they should in the terrible circumstances. The Judge ordered him to tell no-one what he had seen. There had been enough tittle-tattle already. He wanted no more conjecture about what had been going on in the house. The loss of Peter's hand was to be regarded purely as a tragic accident, and the book was to be closed. The doctor nodded anxiously.

Dr Grubb did what he could do to staunch the remaining bleeding, and the servants then carried a delirious Peter downstairs to recover. The doctor, who had never seen such a thing before, took time to examine the severed hand. He asked if he might take it with him for further study.

As strictly ordered by the Judge, Ellen kept the nature of Peter's accident a secret, and sent her children off to school, to protect them as best she could from all that was going on around them. There, at least, they would be safe, under the Reverend Fallowfield's watchful eye.

But even at the school the mood had changed. The children were not so attentive, whispering to each other all the time, and sharing secrets among themselves. The focus of their attention was the grisly talisman which Angel Blake had found in Tarrant's Field, and had kept hidden in her little bag. A glimpse of it caused much chattering in the back row, which, for a while, the Reverend Fallowfield chose to ignore. He was telling them a story from the Old Testament, one which particularly moved him; this storytelling was something he loved to do. On that day, it was the special relationship of Ruth and Boaz, a story of love and faith. He asked the children, 'Why was Boaz thus gentle to Ruth?' hoping they would talk of the spiritual element of the story, of how Boaz's loving care for Ruth echoed God's care for his creation, but they were silent. Only little Mark chirped up with an answer:

'Because he were a man, and she were a woman.'

The other children giggled. They will debase everything, he thought, and threatened them with his cane to bring them to order.

'No, it's mine,' whispered Angel, when one of the other pupils tried to snatch her little bag from her. They did not realise how precious her bag had become to her. At the same time, she wanted to demonstrate its power, and seeing that she was now the centre of attention, she had chosen this moment to begin, slowly, to reveal the contents. It was a large earthy claw, a dark wormy talon, attached by mummified tissue to the first joint of a finger. The pupils who could see it, as she held it carefully below her desk, reacted with noises of alarm and disgust.

'Angela, give me that!' snapped Fallowfield, his patience now at an end. Angel looked at him, all innocence, and as always when she looked him straight in the eye, he began to feel a little nervous.

'Give you what?' she said, secretly returning the talon to its bag and passing it speedily along the row for safe-keeping. She then put both hands on her desk to show that she was hiding nothing. Fallowfield looked for a while at those two open innocent hands and remained silent.

That might have been the end of the affair, but Mark, who now had possession of the bag, could not resist peering into it, and Fallowfield saw him doing so. Angel darted a look of intense fury at Mark, but it was too late.

Fallowfield forced Mark to reveal it, and he now had her precious talisman in his hands.

He began gradually to unwrap the little bag in front of the whole class. The tip of the talon appeared, a maggot wriggling on it, and one of the little girls screamed. This so shocked the Reverend that he fumbled with the bag and dropped it. Instantly it was gone. One of the other pupils had taken it, and it was now being passed around the class from hand to hand behind their backs. Try as he might, the Reverend Fallowfield could not find it again. Suspicion then fell once more upon Mark, who looked guilty, but did not have it.

'They threw'm out the window, Reverend,' he said.

This brought the hunt to a halt, although by then the claw had been secretly returned to Angel. Fallowfield decided not to look further but to call the whole class to account.

'How can you glean any advantage for your souls if you will not listen to the holy writ,' he said. 'The Good Lord himself hath said, "Those that have ears to hear, let them hear!" You gain nothing by playing games with disgusting, heathen fetishes. Listen and learn the truth!'

After the class was over, Angel gathered together a number of her inner circle, including Mark and Cathy, and gave them all a warning.

'No-one is to say one word about what you seen today. There was naught in my bag. The Reverend 'magined it.'

She looked hard at each of them in turn. This was not

the Angel that they knew. A change seemed to have come over her since she found the claw, as if she had become obsessed with it. She was no longer their laughing, bright-eyed companion who was always playing games. She was deadly serious.

'If anyone should tell, and I get to know of it, I shall point yon claw at them, and they will know pain like no other,' she said. Some of the children were very frightened by this, and everyone became silent, but then she relaxed and smiled in a conspiratorial manner, and said, 'Our secret, then?'

They all agreed it was.

Chapter Five

✦ ✦ ✦

The Departure of the Judge

eter awoke from his long sleep to the horrifying fact that his nightmare had been a reality, and the pain was still with him. When she heard his moans from the living room, Ellen hurried to console him, and to bring him some eau de vie. She had sewn for him a leather cover to hide his missing hand. He was not best pleased when he heard the doctor had taken it with him, but what was there to do? Although his hand still throbbed with pain as if it had never gone, it could never be put back in place. Certain things could not be undone. All the same, it took him a long time to realise that he did not have the use of it, and he would stupidly hold out his arm for things he could not reach.

'We get used to everything with time,' said the Judge.

The search for Isobel went on for days, but still it produced only rumours and no result. Cathy was very proud that her Ralph was playing such a prominent role in the hunt for Mistress Banham, even if he could not find her. It was something which had come to involve the entire village. There continued to be sightings of women who looked a little like Isobel, but they all proved incorrect. The stories became ever more fanciful. Some thought the gypsies had taken her. One little girl claimed to have seen her sitting at the top of a huge oak tree, crouching like a bird about to fly away. Squire Middleton's repeated protestations that they were on the right track and would find her soon began to tire and infuriate the Judge more and more. Peter wanted to help the search, but was overtaken by a fever, as his aunt had been, and the doctor had to be called again to his bedside.

Then suddenly – his decisions were always abrupt – the Judge announced that he was needed back in London and must leave straight away. Although they were all afraid of him, the villagers did not want him to go. In their eyes their own Squire and magistrate was a poor deputy to such a man. The Judge had stature. Middleton had not.

As soon as he heard the Judge was going, the Squire decided to call off the search.

'I have given up the chase,' he said. 'There's no trace of the lady anywhere, and it's nine days now.'

'I fear she is lost to us,' replied the Judge, as his coach was made ready for the journey. 'But the doctor is confident,' he added, 'that Mr Edmonton will survive.'

'Ah, the young feller,' said the Squire. 'Then we can be grateful for small mercies.' The Judge nodded.

'I have to leave you now,' he said.

'Of course, affairs of state. Fear not, my lord, the matter is in good hands. I am only sad that you were unable to dine at the manor.'

'I will keep your invitation in mind for another occasion,' the Judge replied, coldly.

Outside in the yard the chickens were squawking and kicking up a noise at the huge horses which had now invaded their space.

'Attend to his lordship,' called the Squire.

At the last minute, Ralph came running up, hoping to catch the Judge before he started on his journey. The 'wise man' was leaving them.

'Your lordship,' he called, 'please don't you desert us, not with things the way they are. We need you here.'

'Squire Middleton has promised to keep good watch over you,' said the Judge as he climbed into his carriage. 'I have important business in London. There are too many villains running wild in that town, and old Tyburn Tree demands to be fed.'

'And you shall spread no more rumours, Ralph Gower,' added the Squire. 'D'ye hear? Fiends in the fields, and suchlike balderdash!'

'Well, perhaps you will have peace from now on, my friends,' said the Judge, making himself comfortable for the journey. Ralph moved away and was joined by Cathy.

'There will be no nonsense here while you're away, my lord,' said the Squire. 'This parish is my family. I am father to all. They love me, but they obey me first.' He followed this with a little chuckle to show he was a generous soul at heart. 'Have a pleasant journey, your lordship.'

Before leaving, the Judge then addressed himself to the Squire and to everyone who had come to see him off. His tone was measured and very serious.

'I will not forget you,' he said, 'but you must learn to have patience, even while people die. Only thus will the whole evil be destroyed. You must let it grow.'

With that he motioned the driver to move off, and the heavy coach with its silent coachman trundled through the farmyard gate and along the deeply rutted road towards London. Lost deep in his own thoughts, the Judge did not cast so much as a single glance back towards the farm and the village that he had left. The Squire mounted his own horse and rode off in a different direction.

Cathy and Ralph watched the Judge's coach as it disappeared into the woodland at the end of the road. He left a feeling of anxiety and uncertainty behind him, as everything had completely changed since his visit. Cathy looked up to the big lad at her side.

'You'll be the man of the house now, Ralph,' she said, 'until the young master is better.' Ralph smiled, but his thoughts were still with the enigmatic words of the Judge, and what they might mean. Let what grow? And who would die?

Chapter Six

✦ ✦ ✦

Children's Games

Peter Edmonton continued to recover, although the loss of Rosalind still weighed upon him, even more heavily than the pain of his lost hand. But the shock of his self-inflicted wound had pulled him from his despondency enough for him to make some decisions. He had the spare room emptied of its ancient furniture and closed up. Some grandiose items from another age wound up in the servants' quarters as a result because they had nowhere else to go. He also decided that he himself would not return to London until his aunt was found or, as now seemed more and more likely, was pronounced dead. He was needed in Chapel Folding.

Ellen Vespers did not like having to live with the contents of the spare room, gilt mirrors and the like, and a huge black chest with runic letters carved into it. She hoped it would not be long before they were sold. She herself had seen something in that room, even before Rosalind arrived, and it was something that she could not easily forget. Another, more immediate worry of hers were the stories which her children told, about how a secret group of schoolchildren had grown up round a girl called Angel Blake, the only daughter of an old tiger of a farm labourer, and how they were all afraid of her.

Mark Vespers was cheeky and impish by nature, and the respect paid to Angel by the other children was to him like a red rag to a bull. He loved riling her, his main method being to tell everyone that the Reverend was sweet on her. But one afternoon his teasing overstepped the mark. He had snatched the leather bag with its precious talisman, which she kept tied round her waist.

'Give it here,' she said sharply, and as she said it, he froze. It seemed as if the claw was moving in its bag. Despite his fear, he managed to taunt her further.

'I knows what you'm get up to, out by yon chapel.'

'Who told you that?'

'Little dicky bird.' He genuinely did not know what he meant. 'Chapel' was just a word he had overheard.

Angel snatched back the claw. 'What kind of bird would that be?'

Freed of the claw, Mark's courage returned to him. 'Can't catch me,' he said, and ran off. Angel did not need to chase after him. She took out the claw, pointing the tip of it towards him as he ran. All at once he was struck by a terrible pain in his leg and collapsed on the ground. He could hear the other children laughing as he limped off towards the woods.

He was still limping and crying when Cathy found him in the copse near the farm. He would tell her nothing about what had happened to him, except that Angel Blake was somehow involved. She put her arm round him so he could hop along, but after a while he let his leg down and refused to move.

'C'mon, Mark,' she said. ''Twon't be long afore yer home.'

After a long while Mark began to hobble on.

'I be alright. It don't hardly hurt no more,' he said defiantly, but it was obvious that he was lying.

'She's a devil, that Angel,' said Cathy. 'She's no friend o' mine.'

''Tweren't her. She likes me,' said Mark, perversely. ''Twere the thing she keeps.'

Cathy now became quite tearful.

'I told 'er she shouldn'ave touched it. Oh Lord, Mark, what shall come of thee?'

Mark tried to explain.

'I done grab the claw, an' Angel were laughin', then sudden-like I had this pain . . .'

'Ssh! Don't tell,' said Cathy. 'Say a prayer. I'll say it with thee.'

They walked on, reciting the Lord's Prayer brokenly, until they reached the farm.

Mark's pain did not go away, and it greatly worried Ellen. She had already heard how Angel and her followers bullied the other children, and had discussed it with many of the mothers, none of whom had dared to complain about it, as if they were afraid of Angel themselves. Now her own children were suffering, and she was not prepared to put up with that. If no-one else would do it, she would speak to Angel herself.

Angel was not hard to find. She was sitting with a group of friends in a field near the old chalk pit, and they were reciting alphabet rhymes, A for this, B for that, and so on, which they must have learnt at school. Each little ditty had a moral purpose, and it was hard to imagine a more innocent scene. There were children there that Ellen knew well, Tom Harker, Winsome Rogers, Tim Parsons, Abi Walters and so on, and she knew their parents too. And there was Angela Blake among them, at the centre of it all.

'Angel Blake, did thou hurt my son?' said Ellen. 'Thou done som'ert to his leg.' Tim Parsons answered for her.

'Your son, Mark, he fell over in a game of tag,' he said, and he was backed up by the others, while Angel sat silently with a smile on her face. They said that Mark had a habit of exaggerating things, which was something Ellen could not deny. She might almost have believed them had not Cathy told her other things about Angel Blake. There was something about Angel's satisfied smile which really provoked her.

'You're to keep away from my children,' she said.

'Why?' asked Angel.

'We like to play with Cathy,' put in Winsome, as if she had been accused.

'If Mark wants to play, why can't he?' said Angel.

'Mark is still unwell. He's not one bit better,' said Ellen, careful to single out Angel from the others. 'What thou done, Angel, is wicked, and much like witchcraft if you were to ask me. The Reverend Fallowfield would not like it one bit if he were to get wind of it.'

The children looked shocked, as if she had suddenly gone mad. There was a long silence before Angel replied.

'That is a terrible thing, Mistress Vespers, calling me a witch. You'll pay for that, twice over.' Angel said this quietly, looking Ellen straight in the eye. The other children ignored Angel's threat as if they hadn't noticed it, or as if it was the most natural thing in the world. They began again with their alphabet rhymes. Ellen looked at them each in turn. They were just children. She had often seen them arguing with each other, shouting and yelling, and that seemed to her more healthy than what she saw now. Angel seemed to have created a strange, controlled harmony among them. She could see there was no point in talking to them anymore. It was their parents and elders who must be told and who should help her. By herself she was out of her depth. With one last look she walked away.

Angel studiously watched her go. What Ellen had said

disturbed her more than she gave out. The term 'witch' still carried a real threat, and only a few years ago, when she was still a child, there had been stories circulating about the hanging of witches in the colonies. On the other hand, she had no fear of the Reverend Fallowfield, because she knew the power she held over him. Whatever he might be told, he would not believe it if she said it was untrue, and he would never hurt her. But Ellen Vespers had to be taught a lesson and kept silent. No-one must get in Angel's way. She had a mission. She had to clear a path for the being who owned the claw, to whom she had given the title 'He Who Is to Come'.

Mark was getting restless. He told his mother his pain had got better, and that he should be allowed out, but she knew that there was still a bad rash on his leg, and it was spreading.

''Tain't nothin', Ma,' said Mark. 'Pain's gone, I promise.' He got up to show her how easily he could do it, but he was still shaky, and she forced him to sit down again.

'You just sit there,' said Ellen, fetching her shawl. 'I'll go find old Dr Grubb. He'll give me some medicine will settle you straight away.' She knew this might be expensive, but she put together all the pennies she could, because she felt it had to be done.

'But, Ma, I be perfect!'

'Hush thee now, I'll be back in a twinkling. Does thou want some soup while I'm gone?'

Mark shook his head.

'Does thou want to go to bed?

'No,' said Mark, horrified at the thought.

'Have an apple,' she then said, as if eating something was the most important thing in life. 'I'll not be long.'

Mark toyed with the apple after she had gone, and took a bite, but it didn't taste so good. He then inspected the rash on his leg. It had begun to grow a kind of fur which disgusted him, and which he did not want his mother to see. He did up his breeches tight to hide it. Out of sight, out of mind. It genuinely did not hurt at present, so he could pretend it wasn't there, and get on with things. He was bored. He took out the box of tricks which he took with him to school and poured out the contents. There was a lump of chalk, some knuckle bones and a feather for a pen, but nothing on which to draw. His marbles ran about, but he could not play marbles on his own. There was the little penknife which he had used to carve his name on the desk in school, but his mother would object strongly if he used it on the kitchen table. In a corner of the kitchen was a big black chest from the spare room, watching him angrily.

He took another bite of the apple and winced with pain. It was then that he noticed there were two young girls looking in at the lattice windows, which Ellen had left half open. He could not tell how long they had been there, because they had been as silent as portraits. One of them he immediately recognised from school. It was Winsome Rogers. The other was an older girl he didn't know. Now that they had his attention, they began to call his name.

'Will thou come and play with us, Mark?' said the older girl, whose name was Dorcas Swift.

'Please,' echoed Winsome.

'You play girls' games,' said Mark, scornfully.

'We don't,' said the girls, speaking almost in unison. 'Anyways, Angel has taught us a new game. Please come.'

Mark thought it over.

'Alright,' he said, after a while. Anything was better than nothing, and it was the perfect excuse to disobey his mother and go out. The sun was shining, and it was a glorious day. He looked at each of the girls in turn. Not his usual playmates, but why not?

Dr Grubb was having a nap, and he did not much like being woken. He lived at the end of the village in an old cottage which had once been one of a row but had long since lost its partners. It leant a little to one side as a result. Ellen knocked persistently at the door, and then explained that her son had a painful rash, but she couldn't tell him why this rash so worried her.

'Have you brought a sample of the boy's urine?' asked the doctor, grumpily. Ellen confessed that it had never occurred to her.

'Pity,' he said. 'One can tell so much by the taste of a sick man's urine.' He thought for a while. 'Was there by any chance some fur connected with this rash?' Ellen was not sure, but she did not think so.

'Good,' said Dr Grubb, 'I'll fetch thee a bottle of my special elixir. That should do the trick. But it's precious. Don't spill a drop.' He disappeared for a moment and soon returned with a bottle of a cure-all which he used for unexplained rashes and a good few other things beside. Ellen showed him her pennies.

'It's all I have,' she said.

'Don't you worry,' said the doctor, taking them. 'But you be sure he gets it all,' and as an afterthought he added, 'and should anything else occur, you let me know.'

Ellen set off through the village very much relieved. She had great faith in the doctor, although, as she went along, she had to confess that she had been just a little perturbed by his last remark. What else might occur? And what had Angel meant, she wondered, when she had said 'twice over'?

Mark found himself in the middle of a clearing in the woods, and there were quite a few children there, boys too. They were playing a game of tag when he arrived. It was near the place where the Reverend Fallowfield had sprained his ankle. Hidden behind the trees were the standing stone and the little ruined chapel. Mark did not know this secret place, and it seemed exciting, as if he were being accepted as an insider into a very special group. There were older boys there too, boys that he looked up to, and they all spoke in hushed tones, as if they did not want to be heard.

A game of 'Blind Man's Buffet' was proposed.

'Who's to be it?'

'Mark's to be it!'

The newcomer was taken and blindfolded. Mark staggered about, his leg now hurting again. He could feel the wind of children running past but could not come near to catching any of them.

'Behind thee! Behind thee!' they called, followed by much laughter. He could hear that the whole group had begun to move away from him, and he followed them as best he could, tripping over stones and brambles. They circled around him for a while, making him dizzy, and then they were off again. He had been lured away for some considerable distance when his outstretched arms felt the ivy at the chapel entrance. He turned and ran straight into the cold hard face of the standing stone. Everything was suddenly quiet.

'Behind thee, Mark!' It was Angel's voice. She pulled the thin, coloured belt from her dress, and from behind him floated a ribbon that unexpectedly tightened strongly round his neck. Angel was now whispering close to his ear.

'He needs thee, Mark.'

Suddenly, she pulled him backwards with the belt, and he was choking. He could hear the other children continuing to play, as if they were unaware of what was happening. In his blindness it seemed as if he and Angel were the only two people in the space in which he now found himself. In the distance he could hear drums were beating, and there was music. The belt, like a sharp ribbon, tightened until he could not breathe at all.

There was a very poor attendance in the Reverend Fallowfield's classroom after lunch that day. As he entered the room, what few pupils there were rose to their feet, with a loud scraping of chairs and creaking of desks. He eyed them with some suspicion as they sat down. Cathy Vespers came in, a little late and out of breath.

'I see that only half my class has deigned to return this afternoon,' said the Reverend. He marched up and down the ranks of desks. The children either looked very prim or very guilty as he walked by. He stopped at Cathy's desk.

'How is Mark?' he asked.

'Better, sir, so I'm told.'

'I'm glad of that. I suppose all these other missing children have unexpectedly succumbed to Mark's distemper?'

His attention was caught by a click at the door, as a girl slunk into the classroom. He followed her with a stony stare until she sat down at her desk, which she did without saying a word. It was Winsome Rogers. She looked up at him, all confusion, as if she had not noticed him before.

'Oh, sorry I's late, Reverend.'

This kind of insolence was something which he did not expect from her.

'I shall speak to you at the end of the lesson,' he said. He returned to his desk and looked around the room, ending with Angel's empty chair.

'Where is Angela Blake?'

The children all looked at each other until Winsome piped up with a prepared speech, in which she gave her best impression of a society lady.

'Angel sends you her respects sir, and says she'm awful sorry that she cannot attend your class . . .' The children began to titter and laugh, which gave her the courage to continue in the same vein.

'But she has some very important things what she must do. She might call by to see thee sometime later, if she ain't too rushed.'

The laughter increased until Fallowfield picked up his cane and smashed it down with considerable force on his desk. His captive grass snake, which was in a glass bowl on the same desk, wriggled in convolutions, desperately attempting to escape.

'Be silent!' yelled Fallowfield with uncharacteristic violence. The class was silent in an instant.

'What is this pernicious infection, this gross ungodliness which is spreading through my class?'

''Tweren't me that said it,' said Winsome in a small voice. 'It were Angel.'

'Yes, it were Angel,' said one of the boys, with a knowing look at his teacher. They all knew that Angel was teacher's pet.

'I cannot understand why she is not here,' said Fallow-field. If all the other children refused to obey him, he still mistakenly felt he could rely on Angel.

On her way back from Dr Grubb, Ellen Vespers encountered Lucy Rogers, the mother of Winsome, and had a long conversation with her, in which she tried to explain to her why she thought that Angel Blake was having a bad effect on the other children, but Winsome's mother would have none of it. She even took Ellen's comments as an attack on her own daughter, and Ellen saw she would get nowhere with her. After wasting too much time in this way, Ellen hurried home, thinking that Mark was still waiting for her, worried that she had left him for too long. She returned by way of the old coppice, which was looking magically beautiful in the dappled sunlight. She found this beauty very comforting in these disturbing times, although now there was something missing from it. It was the singing of the birds. They were strangely silent, as they are supposed to be before a storm, or an eclipse of the sun. She walked on through the silent wood and was close to the farm when she remembered that there was something written on a label attached to the precious bottle which Dr Grubb had given her. Although she was not good at reading, she thought she should try to make sense of it before she gave the elixir to her son. She was just beginning to make out the words when the bottle exploded in her hand.

A stone from a catapult aimed with deadly accuracy had smashed the bottle into pieces. All of Dr Grubb's elixir was lost. Ellen let out a cry. Two young boys, hidden in the bushes, sniggered with glee at what they had achieved.

'Hey, that cost good silver that did. It was for Mark,' shouted Ellen.

One of the boys emerged from his hiding place.

'Save your pains, mistress,' he said. 'Mark won't need it no more.'

Ellen began to walk towards him.

'What mean you, boy?'

'We shut him in the woodshed,' said the boy, and both he and his accomplice then ran away laughing. Ellen began to run after them, but they were far too fast for her. She dropped the last bits of broken glass from her hand and hurried off towards the farm.

'Mark!' she called.

Her fears were confirmed when she discovered that Mark was not where she had left him, and the door was open. She hunted this way and that but there was no sign of him, only a half-eaten apple and the marbles he had left. She was forced to accept that the boys might not have been joking. She came out into the yard and saw Cathy coming home from school.

'Ma, what is it?' she said, seeing the look of panic on her mother's face. But Ellen could not answer.

At the far end of the yard was a sort of lean-to made

of rotting wood, which served as a place for keeping logs. Ellen found that the door was tight shut, but it was so old and battered that it took little effort to force it open. Much to her relief she saw that Mark was not inside, only a big heap of logs. She was on the point of leaving to continue her search elsewhere, when she noticed a piece of cloth caught between two of the logs. It was the same colour brown as Mark's jerkin. She clutched at it, but it would not come away. She pulled away the logs around it, and saw a hand, a child's hand. She dragged away more logs, and there was blood, and more blood, and Mark's crushed and shattered body. A scream caught in her throat for what seemed an age, and then it burst out of her, as she ran for air. Outside, Cathy, who had been watching with alarm, ran up to her, but she pushed her daughter away and forced her into the house, where she herself collapsed on a chair. She was breathing so fast that she almost lost consciousness and her mind was so shaken that she could not properly assimilate what she had just seen. Cathy began to cry.

Chapter Seven

A Visitation

he Reverend Fallowfield often stayed behind after the children had gone, and as he tidied his things away, he pondered the change that had come over his class, considering how he might alter the situation. Could the children's nervous attitude relate to all the stories they had heard about Isobel Banham's farm; how a girl had been taken to the madhouse, how Isobel's nephew had lost his hand in an accident, and how Isobel herself had disappeared? He was aware his pupils had taken a morbid interest in these events, and this seemed to him to be very unhealthy. He felt sorry for little Cathy Vespers that she had been caught up in all that, but she seemed one of the least affected. He remembered the disgusting claw which her little brother Mark had been hiding. What was its significance? It all made no sense, but it deeply disturbed him.

He had been gradually putting together a small collection of animals for his children to study. The latest addition to his collection was a small flea-ridden hedgehog, which was half dead when he found it, but which he had been nursing back to health. Together with the snake, a bird's nest and a rabbit, he hoped he could encourage in the children an interest in the natural world around them. He was dangling a worm in front of the reluctant hedgehog, gently attempting to persuade it to eat, when he heard a hesitant creak, which seemed to come from the heavy door which led into the church. He was not used to people being there at so late an hour. Slowly the door opened. He felt a chill wind as if the devil himself were about to enter the room. But it was a young girl's voice that spoke.

'Fallowfield.' The voice was both soft and arrogant at the same time. 'I'm so glad you're still here.'

For Lucian Fallowfield it was as if a ghost had spoken, but the heavy door now opened fully to reveal the white figure of Angel Blake, wearing only a night shift. She walked towards him slowly and a little awkwardly. He was deeply surprised but reacted with nervous dignity.

'I . . . I've been meaning to speak to you, Angel. You address me as "Reverend".'

'I'm not in school now . . . Reverend.'

'Your behaviour, Angel, has been most unseemly of late. I mean to complain to your father about it . . .' Fallowfield realised that he was still holding the hedgehog and hid it away in his desk. Angel took advantage of this moment to undo the front of her shift and allow it to fall from her shoulders. When Fallowfield let down the desk lid and looked up, he was rendered speechless.

'Do you like me, sir?' The shift now fell to the ground, and she stood there, completely naked. 'Do you like what you see?' Fallowfield was amazed how womanly she had become. She was fifteen and no longer a little girl. He was like a man spellbound. The attraction he felt for her body was almost more than sexual. It held a supernatural fascination for him, as if he were already there, with her in his arms, in some dream world.

'Shame on you, child,' he stammered. 'Cover yourself this instant.' He remembered the story of Saint Dunstan, who was visited by the devil in the guise of a beautiful woman while he was working at his forge. Saint Dunstan knew it was the devil because she had a cloven hoof hidden beneath her skirts, and he had grabbed her by the nose with his red-hot tongs. Angel, however, had no hint of a cloven hoof. Her feet were perfect, as was the whole of her body, and for being naked she seemed all the more innocent, and pure, and lovely. She was no devil. She never could be.

'Do you like what you see?' she repeated.

'You . . . you are beautiful, Angel,' said the priest. He could say nothing else.

'Do you want to play our games with us?' said Angel.

This was too much. Fallowfield regained a little of his composure.

'No . . . no. Cover yourself up.'

'We want you with us . . . sir.'

'Cover yourself! The Lord have mercy on you!'

'Come with me . . .' She moved closer and took his hand. For a moment he allowed himself to be pulled towards her, but he resisted the urge to touch her naked body and pushed her away with closed fists. Having broken the spell, his anger welled up, and he slapped her across the face. She backed away for a moment, but then looked up, indignant, hurt and shocked, her eyes piercing straight into his.

'For shame!' he said. 'Be gone with you, hussy. I do not ever wish to see you in my class or in this school again!'

For a second, she looked at him with undisguised venom, but then she smiled, as if she enjoyed his anger.

'Would you like to know,' she said, 'what happens to your pupils? Well, one of them is dead already. Little Mark had the devil in him, so we cut it out!'

With this she snatched up her shift and stalked out of the room, the heavy door swinging closed behind her, its cold wind leaving a shattered Fallowfield struggling to understand the full meaning of her words. He had loved that girl. She was his ideal pupil. For her to turn against him seemed to cast suspicion even on the God he worshipped. He walked shakily across to the open window to watch her delicate form disappearing among the stones of the graveyard and into the night.

As she walked through the woods towards her home, Angel felt bitter and angry. It would have been a great victory to have seduced a man of the cloth, and one who was forever preaching high morality. She was still a virgin, and she had offered him everything. She would have committed her first carnal act with him, forcing him to join her in sin. Her Master would have been so pleased with her. But she had been deprived of her victory and had also been forced to quash her own sexual arousal. 'That man was even more bloodless than I imagined,' she told herself by way of consolation. 'What use is he?'

She sought out a thorn bush, and deliberately walked into it, making sure the thorns drew blood. In her growing rage she went even further, hurting herself badly and spraying the excess blood over the front of her shift. After she had pierced and cut herself with the thorns, she smeared mud on her face. She then set off for her cottage where she knew her father would be waiting for her.

Bill Blake was a man so full of anger and grievances that he always had something to be indignant about. He could not live without his fury at the world. On this night it was his daughter, who was not coming home when she should. She had been out far too long. His anger only increased when he saw her approaching the cottage wearing nothing but a shift. What in the name of God had the girl been doing? He grabbed her fiercely by her arm and dragged her indoors.

But Angel knew her father, and she knew how to control him. She burst into floods of tears and said the clothes had been taken from her. He then let her go, and looked at her, and for the first time he saw the blood.

'There weren't nothing I could do,' she said. 'He be stronger than I.' He now knew why she had been so late, and he forgave her instantly. It had dawned on him that his daughter had been raped, but he did not yet know which boy had done it, and who should be beaten for it. He tried to get from her who was responsible, but she simply broke down in more tears and would not give a name. It was only after some considerable time and many threats that the word 'Reverend' slipped out. Even Bill, who was always ready to take issue with the world, was shocked into silence. He had thought it was a boy, surely not an older man, not a priest! He brought his fist down with such force that it almost broke the table in two.

Chapter Eight

The Burial

he crows were gathering again over Tarrant's Field when Peter Edmonton went to inform the Squire of the death of Ellen Vespers' son. Ellen had only recently nursed him back to health, but now the roles were reversed, and Peter had to look after her in her grief, to console her in all her pain after the terrible death of her son and try to make some sense of it. Circumstances had altered everything in his life, and from being a bookish, pen-pushing law student he had suddenly become a gentleman farmer, something for which he felt completely unsuited, but, as he told the Squire, he was prepared to take on most things and learn. Helping to run the farm and participating in some physical labour himself had a curative effect, although he had to confess that the horror of this latest atrocity was almost too much for him.

'Too much for you, eh?' said the Squire. 'Well, it is not too much for me!' Squire Middleton, who had given up the hunt for Isobel Banham with some relief after the Judge had gone, found himself galvanised into action by this new case. He listened with growing horror and anger to the details of it.

'I am for the most part a tolerant man,' he said, 'but there is one thing I cannot tolerate, and that is attacks upon children.'

The Squire had always wanted a son of his own, but his overbearing wife, his Joan, had proved barren. It was one of the tragedies of his life that he had no-one to teach or to take over his estates, and the murder of a young boy held for him a particularly bitter taste. He took it upon himself, as a matter of urgency, to discover the cause of the boy's death, and find the culprit, which he assured everyone he would surely do, and when he did there would be hell to pay. He asked for Mark's corpse to be laid before him, and puzzled over it for a while with sadness and confusion. It was the large wound on the boy's leg that attracted most of his attention, and that, he declared, must be the cause of his death. He completely ignored the bruises on his neck, and, as was his way, he jumped to the first conclusion that fitted.

'It must be a wild beast,' he said. 'We have too many wild pigs in our woodland, and they must be hunted and killed.'

Peter gently dismantled this theory. If it was a wild beast, why did that beast go to the length of hiding the body under a pile of wood in a shed?

'Perhaps it was building some sort of nest there.'

'And that in a farmyard, with nobody noticing?'

Squire Middleton had to admit even to himself that perhaps he had been a little hasty, but he had not wanted to consider the other possibility, that there had been a human hand involved. All the same, he was slowly forming a new opinion. The death of this boy had to be the work of a man, perhaps the same man who had been behind other terrible events in the village. Perhaps this man had killed Isobel Banham and hidden her body. Perhaps he had even cut off young Edmonton's hand in his sleep.

'I will find the villain,' he said, 'and he shall pay for this.' Middleton was also forming an idea as to who this villain might be, but he could not yet prove anything.

His theory was soon backed up by the evidence that others found. Dr Grubb declared the cause of Mark's death to be asphyxiation, with something very thin, like a child's belt or a ribbon. Two young boys had predicted to Ellen Vespers where Mark's body was to be found. How did they know? Everything seemed to lead back to that damned school next to the church, and by implication to the man who ran the classes there, and who had somehow perverted the minds of all the children in the village. The Squire had long believed that the highly principled Reverend Fallowfield was too good to be true. On many occasions he had tried to persuade him to become more human, but Fallowfield had always taken the moral high ground. Now he was beginning to believe that Fallowfield could never have been human at all. He was a monster. Of course, he could not say this outright. There were a lot of people who still respected their vicar. But the day would come when he would be unmasked. The Squire was now sure of it.

A single bell tolled. The Reverend Fallowfield himself conducted the service with great gravity, as Mark's small body, wrapped in rough hessian, was lowered into the ground. There was quite a large group of mourners, including Mark's family, the other members of the Banham household, Ralph Gower, the Squire himself, and Peter Edmonton. Everyone had been shocked by the death of this poor son of a serving woman, and it had drawn sympathy from much of the village, both the parents and the children.

Halfway through the service, Cathy was alarmed and distressed to see that Angel Blake was quietly joining the group. She told her mother, who fixed Angel with a stony stare. However, despite her animosity, she could not do so for long before a new wave of grief overcame her, and she shook with tears. Although she had grown to hate Angel, she could not really believe that she, a young girl, had been responsible for Mark's death. There must be another cause.

Angel smiled inwardly, knowing that she now had total power over the Vespers family. She took the claw from her bag and pointed it at her former friend, Cathy. Cathy winced with pain and clutched her side. Seeing this, Ralph moved closer to support her and, before she could be noticed, Angel turned away. She was then joined by her father, who stood next to her, staring at the Reverend Fallowfield from beneath his bushy eyebrows with undisguised hatred. His desire to interrupt the service and throw the priest into the grave that he was praying over was enormous, but Angel held him back. She whispered to him that it made no sense to attack the priest directly. They must make their complaint through the official channels. She indicated the serious and self-important figure of the Squire.

Winsome Rogers and her friend Dorcas watched the burial as silently as they had once watched Mark through the kitchen window, although Winsome's friend could not resist a smiling glance at Angel. Angel did not respond but looked piously at the ground. Fallowfield did not fail to notice Angel's presence as he continued the service, and it made him very nervous indeed.

'Dust thou art, and unto dust thou shalt return . . .'

The token handful of earth was thrown on the body, and finally he closed his prayer book and placed it on his big black Bible. The moment this happened, and before she could say anything, Angel was grabbed from behind by Cathy, who took hold of her hair.

'How durst thou!' she screamed. 'How dare thou show thyself at my brother's grave, thou evil vixen!' Everyone was very shocked at this. 'Thou put a curse on him, thou did! He suffered 'cause of thee!'

Fallowfield felt that he ought to intervene, but he was afraid of possible consequences, and did so very ineffectually. Peter was amazed. It was a side of Cathy he had never seen, but if she felt like that, there must surely be a reason. In the end it was the Squire who had to raise his stick to force the fighting girls apart. Angel immediately clung to her father as if she had been the injured party. Fallowfield was very annoyed by this, and tried to speak to the Squire, who ignored him completely. It was Bill Blake who took all his attention.

'That young bitch attacks my child,' he roared, 'after all she'm been through! Aren't she suffered enough?'

'What is this?' asked the Squire.

'Call that man a priest?' he said, pointing at Fallowfield. 'He's a devil!'

'No, Father,' protested Angel, 'you mustn't . . .' but then she collapsed in a cascade of fake tears.

Bill Blake pulled himself up to his full height. The Squire was paying attention to him now. He felt important.

'Sir, I wish to report a gross misdemeanour concernin' my child.'

'Ach, that was just a tussle between young girls,' said the Squire.

'No, sir, it were last night . . .'

'Oh, Pa . . .' whimpered Angel.

'The Squire must be told,' said Bill.

Perhaps ill-advisedly, Fallowfield tried to intervene. 'Squire . . .'

'What is it?' snapped the Squire. Fallowfield stammered, unable to think how to phrase the delicate things he had to say. Meanwhile Angel was watching Cathy from beneath her dishevelled hair. She was suffering badly from the pain in her side, and Angel secretly pointed her claw again to make it worse.

'What ails thee, love?' Ralph was asking as they walked away. In this, at least, Angel was triumphant.

'If I might have a talk,' said Fallowfield, 'in private, later.' He could not speak in front of Angel. The Squire nodded his agreement, and the Priest reluctantly backed away. As soon as he was gone, Angel found her voice.

'He's no true man of God,' she said. 'He called me back after class yesterday, 'cause he said I'd been doing wrong, and then he asked me to take my dress off, seeing as I had to be punished. I didn't obey, sir, but then he laid his hand upon me. I tried to run away but he caught me, and tore my dress apart . . . I were so afeard.' She then began to cry bitterly.

'She had naught on but a shift when she came home, sir,' said Bill Blake, 'and she were bleeding.'

The Squire was deeply shocked, but he also felt justified. This was exactly the evidence he needed to confirm the suspicions he had held all along. He had doubted himself until then, but not anymore. Angel then went further.

'He told me if I didn't obey him, the same'd happen to me as had to Mark. I didn't know what he meant, sir. I'm scared. What'll I do?'

'And this man had the effrontery . . .' spluttered the Squire. He looked around to strike Fallowfield with his stick, but he had already gone.

'Be damned,' he said. 'In the name of heaven, I'll put an end to your games, Reverend Fallowfield!' With this he bustled out of the graveyard, waving his stick in the air. 'Men!' he called.

Fallowfield was caught by the Squire's servants before he even got as far as the rectory. He was tied with a rope and dragged like an animal to the village lock-up, before anybody could see what was happening and protest or intervene. For the Squire, the case had now been solved, and it only remained for the verdict to be delivered. Justice had moved fast.

Ellen and her daughter returned to the farm, unaware of all this, and with no knowledge of what had happened to the priest. They came back to a painful feeling of emptiness.

'God willing, the Squire will find the murderer soon,' said Ellen.

'I can't forget what she did,' said Cathy, still thinking of Angel. 'She had no respect.'

'Don't thou dwell on it,' was Ralph's response. 'Think . . . We must see the crops sown and cared for, or there'll be nothing for us all to eat come winter. I'll be working full hard today. Mister Peter depends on me.' This was his best homespun philosophy. Life must go on, no matter what.

'Take care of yourself, Cathy my dearest.' He gave her a kiss and went out.

'There, did you see, Ma?' said Cathy through her tears. 'It's not everyone he calls "my dearest" like that, is it, Ma?'

Ellen did not reply. Her daughter seemed so vulnerable,

and she was crying helplessly. She wiped her eyes and took Cathy in her arms.

'Oh, we are a couple of silly blockheads,' she said. Her only way of coping with tragedy was to belittle it. She then began to prepare the kitchen and handed Cathy a bowl which was taking up room where she wanted to work.

Outside in the fields, Ralph discovered that spring had sneaked up on him without his noticing, and the bushes were strewn and burgeoning with flowers. He remembered how this special beauty always seemed to happen in times of mourning, such as the day his father died. God and the angels are trying to compensate, he thought. The sun shines particularly brightly on such a day.

When the Squire next met with Peter Edmonton, he was cock-a-hoop that he had solved the big mystery that was hanging like a dark cloud over Chapel Folding.

'I have the man,' he said. Peter enquired who it was and was very surprised to find that it was the priest, a man whom he had always found to be genuine and friendly, if a little shy, and someone that he truly liked.

'Now the Bishop shall have him trussed up like a chicken, and that'll be an end to his devilry,' said the Squire.

'But can you really be sure you have the right man?' said Peter. 'I can't believe it of him, not Fallowfield. I could as much believe it was the children.'

'I have evidence,' retorted the Squire, not wanting to repeat the details of Angel's story. 'Fallowfield has been the cause of all the evil things that have recently beset our village. I have felt it in my bones for a long time.'

Squire Middleton had always claimed that he did not believe in black magic, but he did believe that Fallowfield exerted a baleful influence over children and events that was somewhere akin to black magic. Yes, he was the cause of everything.

'Has he confessed?' asked Peter. The Squire found this question uncomfortable because the Reverend Fallowfield had done nothing but protest his innocence from the moment he was arrested.

'He will,' was his reply, 'and when he does so, I will bring you chapter and verse. I didn't believe it myself at first, but now I've smelt him out, and netted him, this Minister from Hell.'

After his encounter with Peter, the Squire was forced to admit to himself that, although as magistrate he could act as judge and jury, his victory was not complete until he had a signed confession from the priest, and that he resolved to get. Without it, his judgement would be questioned, if not now, then later.

He went himself to the village lock-up, a tiny space next to a high wall which had been used for that purpose for longer than people could remember, and he ordered that Fallowfield be taken from his cell and brought to the woodshed where he believed that Mark had been murdered, hoping that if he revisited the scene of his crime, he might break down and confess.

Fallowfield said he did not recognise the place, nor the

axe which was put into his hand as being a likely murder weapon, even though no blood was ever found on it.

'How did it feel,' said the Squire, 'when you had that axe in your hand and the small boy trembling at your feet?'

'I loved the boy,' said Fallowfield. 'I would never hurt him.'

'I intend to make an example of you for all the world to see, and to cleanse our village of the infamy you have brought upon us.'

Fallowfield was unable to keep silent any longer. He would tell the truth.

'You misunderstand,' he pleaded. 'It was Angel. She came to the schoolroom at night and attempted to frighten me with stories about Mark Vespers. I will not say what else she did, but . . .'

'What else did she do?'

'She boasted that she and some other children had caught and killed the boy.'

'Children?! Are you trying to blame your crimes on children? What kind of a monster are you?'

'I do not say the children were to blame,' said Fallowfield. 'They were not, but they were possessed.'

This was too much for the Squire.

'I will not hear any more of this nonsense. Take him back to the lock-up and flog him until he tells the truth.' When he remembered the state of Mark's body, the Squire would gladly have taken up the whip himself.

He warned his men firmly, 'Only come to me when

you have done your work and he has confessed fully. Then I will listen, but only then.'

He stalked out, leaving his men to wield their whips, which they did very thoroughly.

His back now bleeding, and in terrible pain, Fallowfield tried to lessen the horror of it by prayer. He inwardly compared his condition to that of the innocent Christ who was also flogged, telling himself that he must bear his wounds as Christ had done. Christ had not confessed to anything, and neither would he. The men were amazed. They had never met a soul who would not confess to killing his mother and his grandmother too under such duress. They could not go back to the Squire with nothing to tell him, but they decided they would give their aching arms a rest, and so they shut the cell door.

Fallowfield was on his knees. He did not know how long he would be able to endure what was happening to him, but he also knew that beyond all else the truth must be heard, or other children would suffer. He prayed devoutly that the Squire would see sense, and that Angel, his sweet Angel, would shake off her bedevilment, and return to the innocent young girl she once had been.

He sat dejected for days. There was only one small, barred window in his cell which was set high in the wall. Through that small aperture sunlight was streaming. Standing on the rickety bed, he could only just reach it, and he could not stay there for long, hanging by his fingers from the stone wall, but there he could catch a glimpse of the outside world and the freedom which he had so suddenly lost. He could see three young women coming along the road. One was wearing a flowery head-dress, and had her head bowed. The other two he recognised. They were the Downes sisters, Rachel and Margaret. When the girl in the headdress looked up, he was amazed to see that it was Angel herself. It was like a vision. The Downes sisters were in their twenties, older than Angel, and he knew them to be devoted members of his congregation. Margaret had made a wonderful job of decorating the church for the harvest festival in the preceding year. They could only be a good influence on the younger girl. He began to wonder if the miracle he had prayed for had actually occurred, and that Angel had repented. The story of her seduction by the devil would be told as an example to the whole parish. The women were discussing it already, and he would soon be released.

This fantasy did not last long. Angel turned and looked in his direction. Whether she knew he was there or had just guessed it, he could not tell, but it was not a friendly glance, and when he looked into her piercing eyes, all the strength went out of his hands. He could support himself no longer and fell. As he sat on the bed in the shadow, he thought for a moment about the headdress she was wearing. Although it was covered in flowers, it was a crown of thorns she wore, and it seemed to him like a terrible sacrilege. He felt that he himself was now wear-ing a crown of thorns, and his head was dripping blood.

Chapter Nine

✦ ✦ ✦

The Ceremony of Spring

athy asked her mother if she could go and collect some wildflowers for her brother's grave. Ellen did not like the idea of her going off into the woods alone, but it was such a beautiful day that it was hard to say anything against it.

'I'm not 'tall sure 'tis safe,' was all she said.

'There's still some Lenten lilies and primroses, I've seen, and all the bushes are in flower. Which field is Ralph a-workin'?'

'I couldn't tell thee.'

'Couldn't I look for'm?'

'Well, if thou'rt really heart-set on it,' said Ellen, 'but don't you wander far.' The fact that Cathy and Ralph would soon meet up set her mind at rest and did something to allay the sense of foreboding she had recently developed about those woods and what might be hiding there.

Cathy could not find Ralph in the fields, as he was working with a cart some way off, but the woodland offered rewards beyond her wildest dreams. All the flowers of early spring were there, and she was soon knee-deep in them. The primroses had gone but the May bushes were already in full bloom, and they snowed the air with petals if you brushed them. It seemed like paradise on earth, and Cathy was drunk with the scent and beauty of it. She helped herself to some purple sage and was looking around for some flowers with longer stems to accompany it, when two boys suddenly appeared, one on either side of her, from out of the flowering bushes. She was shocked at first, but then she recognised them: Tim Parsons and Will Courtenay. They were not her particular friends, but they were fellow pupils in the schoolroom. They were not strangers. Had she known it, they were the same two boys who had waylaid her mother on the day that Mark died, but to Cathy they were friendly and helpful. Will was something of an acrobat and liked to lark about. He could hang upside down from a tree branch, holding on with his legs.

'Have you seen Ralph Gower?' she asked, but neither of them had.

'Those are fine flowers,' said Tim. 'Who are they for?'

'For my brother, to put upon his grave.'

'Oh, poor Cathy,' said Will. 'We was so sad about your Mark.'

'Yes, poor Mark,' repeated Tim.

'Tell thee what,' said Will, 'I know where there are some giant clumps of flowers with fine long stems.'

'Are they far away?' said Cathy.

'Not far.'

The two boys led her further into the woods, circling around her, laughing and playing games. They lifted her together over a small hill of brambles. She quite enjoyed all the attention she was getting, although she wondered why.

Ralph was still some distance away, having stopped his cart to remove a stone from his horse's hoof, but he could hear their laughter in the distance. Then he heard a girl scream, which worried him for a moment, but then there was laughing again. It was only children playing games. It was a beautiful day for it.

The two boys each had hold of Cathy's hands as they walked along. Tim was carrying her bunch of flowers.

'Where are we going?' Cathy asked.

'To a secret place,' said Tim.

'Where we dance, and play our games,' said Will.

'You said we wouldn't go far.' It seemed to be becoming a long, long way.

'Look!' said Tim suddenly, and Cathy looked where he pointed with great alarm, but there was nothing there. While she was looking, Will climbed the tree behind them. To Cathy it appeared as if he had completely vanished. She was searching around for him, when he jumped down, right on top of her, linking his arms round her neck.

'Let me go!'

'It's just a game,' said Will. 'We're cannibals and you're our captive. Quickly, where's the rope?'

Tim fished an old piece of rope from the undergrowth, which, by some strange coincidence, he knew to be there. Both boys began to twist the rope around Cathy.

'You're hurting me,' cried Cathy. 'Ow! Mind my side! You're too rough. You can play by yourselves. I have to go home.'

The boys loosened the rope.

'Sorry, Miss Cathy,' said Tim, apologetically.

Cathy was reminded how sore her back had become since Mark's funeral, when Angel had pointed the claw at her. She felt up inside her blouse, and her hand came up against fur, fur which was never there before. She was now very scared. She was terrified the boys might see it. Did it really belong to her? Her face was white, and Will was aware of it.

'Please will you come with us,' he said, 'if we promise to be gentle? Just for a little?'

Cathy was clutching her back, trembling. 'Alright, but only for a little while, and remember I'm a girl.'

The boys were delighted again and began to stage mock fights between each other as they walked along.

*

Ralph had been driving his rough old cart on a lane through the woods nearby, but the road turned away, and he could no longer hear any sound of children. He then noticed Peter Edmonton walking towards him and took off his hat.

'Do you know that Cathy Vespers is looking for you?' asked Peter.

'No, sir.'

'Mistress Ellen told me so.'

'I heard some children laughing some while ago. I thought it sounded a bit like Cathy, but I've not seen her.'

'Ellen said she was alone,' said Peter.

'Alone?' Alarm bells sounded in Ralph's head. She had not been alone. The other children. The scream. Without time for any explanation, Ralph leapt from his cart and headed off into the woods, leaving Peter bewildered and in charge of his horse. He could hear Ralph calling.

'Cathy! Cathy!'

Cathy did not hear him. The boys had already led her far away, into the clearing by the standing stone.

'I don't like it here,' she said, 'and there aren't no flowers. You lied to me.' The boys just laughed.

'You can't go now,' they said, 'not now.'

Cathy tried to run away but discovered she had been caught around her ankle by their rope. As the noose tightened, she fell flat on her face.

'Oh pardon, Cathy. Beg pardon.' It was a third boy who spoke, someone who she hadn't seen was there. At the same time, she was aware of other voices not far off, chanting to the beat of a drum.

'Here she is,' said Tim. 'She's come for us.'

Cathy looked towards the standing stone with the chapel behind it, and saw Angel approaching, clothed completely in white, wearing her hawthorn headdress. She carried a second headdress high in front of her. The singing voices now all chanted the name 'Cathy!'

'Welcome, Cathy,' said Angel as she placed the second headdress on Cathy's head. Cathy, terrified, had no choice but to accept the crown, as the boys had closed ranks behind her. It was an old ceremony which on the surface seemed similar to the crowning of the Queen of the May, but which was in other ways quite different. The boys lifted her into the air, and she could see that inside the chapel there was a whole group of people waiting for her. The music and the chanting continued, the drumbeat becoming more and more insistent.

'Where be you taking me?' she cried. 'Let me go!' Cathy twisted herself to break free, but she could not hope to reach the ground, and she realised that her struggles were fruitless. There were far too many of them for her to think of escaping. Like some victorious yet helpless heroine, she was being carried through the air in their hands. Still her name was being called, and then, quite unexpectedly, something inside her said, 'Let them. Let them do to me what they will do to me.' She was special. She was the chosen one. She was indeed the

Queen of the May, and even if being special meant that she must die like a mayfly, queen for a day, it was still a magnificent feeling. She had become an integral part of the grand ceremony which the continual chanting invoked, a ceremony which seemed to have come from the beginning of time, and she was almost ecstatic, as if she were floating outside her body. It is said that when an antelope is in the jaws of a lion and is being eaten alive, there comes a point when it no longer tries to escape, but becomes peaceful and quiet, and calmly obedient to fate. This was how Cathy felt at that moment. It did not last long.

Ralph thought he could hear strange chanting in the distance, but the wind took the sound away again, and he could not tell where it was coming from. He called out time and again, 'Cathy! Cathy!' but he got no reply. He went chasing madly in different directions in the false hope of finding her, hearing noises from this place and that, until he was completely lost. His only signpost was a thin column of hazy smoke, which he thought must come from Ned Carter's charcoal mound. He ran towards it and, having discovered that his supposition was correct, he asked Ned, his only hope, if he had seen some children going by, or if he had seen Cathy.

'They go up there,' said Ned, pointing to a place which was not so far from where Ralph had just been. 'There were some came by just now!' he added. 'That's where they play their games; I seen 'em, in the old chapel by the Currell Stone.' Ralph did not pause to ask what the 'Currell Stone' was, but ran off as fast as he could in the direction that Ned had indicated.

Cathy broke from her dream world and was full of ice-cold fear again. A fire was burning. She could hear Margaret Downes intoning some kind of incantation, the meaning of which she did not at first understand. It seemed to be a prayer to some being she called 'the Master'.

'Our Master Behemoth, the great beast of the woodland. Rise now, from the forest, from the furrows. Take thou my blood, my skin, my flesh, and walk.'

What was Margaret doing there, saying such things? The people with her, they were not just children. There were village folk of all ages, some old and wizened, all following the chant with strange smiles on their faces. Then she saw her mistress among them, Isobel Banham, back, it seemed, from the dead. Cathy called out to her for help, but Isobel's eyes had glazed over, paying no attention to anything but the chanting. She could see there was a hideous wound on her shoulder. Where was Mister Peter, and Rosalind Barton? Would no-one help her?

Many of those present had scars and wounds and some had missing limbs, yet they cheered and they chanted, calling 'Cathy' all together, as if they had no minds of their own, only the terrible general purpose of following the dark ritual. Hands were pawing at her from all sides, reaching for the fur which she now knew to be growing on her back. They tore the clothes from her, stripping and shredding them to pieces. The men grew close, rough men of all ages, and she knew that those who wanted would have their way with her. She saw in the faces of all those watching that whatever happened to her, none would move to save her. They would all chant and relish it. She closed her eyes and tried to believe she was dreaming, thinking only of Ralph, and the love that they had never fully known together. She thought how it might have been when she gave herself to him at last on their wedding day, her true lover, while these vile creatures were tearing her apart.

Then there was a sound like thunder, and a voice deeper and more terrible than any she had ever heard before, a voice which seemed to come from the ground, as if it were the voice of the earth itself, spoke and said,

'She has my skin!'

All at once there were screams of terror and ecstasy from everyone around her. She was thrown up and turned over and fell flat into the arms of one of the men, the appointed one, and he had hold of her, and all the noises seemed to go far away. Angel stepped forward with a pair of old sheep shears in her hand, as if she meant to shear the hair from Cathy's back, even as she was violated. She paused with the shears in the air, and then a look of infernal hatred overcame her, and she plunged the shears into Cathy's back again and again, licking the blood from them before she began to reclaim the skin of her Master.

When Ralph finally reached the clearing with its standing stone, there was nobody to be seen. The whole crowd had vanished, and the place felt unnaturally silent, although on the ground was evidence of the many feet which had recently been dancing there. The disappearance of these dancers made the place feel even more desolate. He walked through the crackling undergrowth to the ivy-covered entrance of the ruined chapel and let out a terrible howl. A fire had recently been put out, and in the ashes lay the half-naked body of a young girl. Although she lay face down, he knew who it was.

His whole simple world and all his happiness collapsed around him. He looked up into the bright clear sky and remembered his thoughts about the strange brightness which followed times of mourning. It now seemed to him that all the angels in heaven were weeping in that bright blue sky, as they looked down upon that little blood-stained body lying there in all its desperate, helpless loneliness. Why had he not been there to save her?

'Cathy!!!'

Peter stood by Ralph's rickety cart, waiting for him to return. He thought he had only gone for a little while, but a long time passed and there was still no sign of him. He then heard a cry from the woodland, but he did not know what it meant until Ralph came staggering through the trees carrying the body of a young girl in his arms.

'Oh God!' he cried. The nightmare was still with them. Feeling quite numb, he helped Ralph lift Cathy on to the old cart, and together they set out for the village, not stopping until they reached the manor house.

The Squire was shattered and could barely hide his horror when he saw Cathy's little body covered in blood. It was clear that the poor girl had been ritually murdered. The killing had continued, and he had been unable to do anything to prevent it. His pride was destroyed, as was his sense of order. He was no longer in control of the parish, and he had no idea what might happen next. When she was alive, his wife had questioned everything he said or did, and now she was dead he had hopes that he could prove himself right at last, but now his greatest theory had apparently been wrong. He had solved nothing, and the murders went on.

He paced around in a pointless fury. It took them a long time to shake him from the idea that Lucian Fallowfield was in some way responsible, even though all the time he had been in the lock-up. For a while he thought that he must have found some way of controlling people from inside his cell, and was still in favour of hanging him as an example to others. It took all the powers of persuasion of both Ralph and Peter to talk him out of it. Ralph told him where he had found the body, and about the old chapel and the so-called Currell Stone which stood nearby. He said that although he had personally seen no children, he had definitely heard them in the woods. Peter backed him up in this, as he also had heard children's laughter and cries. The Squire was silent.

Peter then outlined his own theory, that what had happened to Cathy was part of some arcane and sadistic ritual which had the old standing stone at its centre. She had been a sacrificial victim, and, unwittingly or not, the children had played a part in it. Although his whole understanding was against it, this theory began to get through to the Squire, and it offered him a new course of action. This murderous ceremonial had to be stamped out at its source, and he was the man to do it. But he still could not entirely be shaken from the idea that Fallowfield was in some way involved in the ritual.

'He was not!' said Peter, but there was no arguing with the Squire. It was pointless.

Peter knew where he could find the only person who could deal with the dark shadow that had overtaken the village. Judge Nathan Mandeville had predicted that the threat would grow, and had promised to return. He was a man of great knowledge and had seen crimes of all kinds. The village could no longer survive without him. Peter did not want to offend the Squire by suggesting he had dealt badly with the problem, as he knew that the Squire was very sensitive about any suggestion that he had made a mistake. He also knew that Fallowfield's life might depend on humouring him. So, he quietly returned to the farm, called the groom, saddled his big white horse, and set off at speed for London.

Chapter Ten

✦ ✦ ✦

The Groaning Stone

efore he would let him free, the Squire summoned Fallowfield for one last round of questioning. He asked him what he knew of the rituals which took place in the chapel in the woods, where Cathy's body had been found.

'Do you know that place?' he asked. 'Have you been there?' Fallowfield confessed that he did know of the existence of the chapel and its standing stone.

'The Currell Stone,' put in the Squire. Fallowfield did not know the name, but he had felt it was an evil place.

So Fallowfield did know. Earlier, his confession might have meant the death penalty, but the Squire now needed the priest for another purpose.

'The man has had punishment enough,' he said, half to himself. 'Release him!'

He then warned Fallowfield that if he stepped out of

line once more, it would mean the rope. Fallowfield, now a broken man and frightened, knew better than to continue with his claim that he had been innocent all along, and let the matter rest.

Squire Middleton had a plan. If he could not find the invisible worshippers of the evil cult which had taken root in Chapel Folding, he could at least destroy their place of worship. When they knew that their ritual stone had been broken, and their chapel levelled, they would either give up their murderous beliefs or move elsewhere, and not bother him anymore. He assembled a group of his strongest men, with rope and tackle, to remove the standing stone. The Reverend Fallowfield was now also needed to exorcise and bless the place. Fallowfield protested that, not being a Catholic, he had never performed an exorcism, but the Squire would not take no for an answer. Now that he had been reinstated, his blessing was required.

'I don't believe in your damned exorcisms anyway,' said the Squire privately, 'but the villagers must.'

Ralph begged not to be one of those tasked with removing the stone, as the memory of what he had seen there was still too strong with him. After some debate, this permission was reluctantly granted. When the day came, the Squire also did not go, as although he would never admit to it, there was enough superstitious fear still left in him to make him feel safer if he remained at home.

It was a cloudy day when the work party arrived in the clearing and dug away at the earth around the Currell Stone, which proved almost as hard as rock. They tied their ropes around the craggy waist of the monolith. Trembling, Fallowfield began his '*Exorcizo te* . . .' and as soon as he did so, the wind got up. It began with a great roaring in the distance, and the sky darkened. Despite this, the men pulled on their ropes and the great stone began to move. As it moved, it gave off a sound as if it were groaning in pain. It seemed as if its roots were being tugged agonisingly from the ground, and they uttered a hideous moaning sigh which grew and grew in intensity until the workmen could no longer bear it. This groaning was heard from miles away. In the village they heard it. The Squire heard it. Ellen Vespers heard it. Ralph heard it. Ned Carter heard it, and all around. The workmen on the site dropped their ropes and ran off in terror, convinced they were being pursued, leaving the Currell Stone leaning at an angle.

Only the Reverend Fallowfield remained, rooted to the spot in a state of shock. He could not continue with the service of exorcism, and let his prayer book fall to the ground. Feeling as if he had lost his last support, he sensed a dark, malign presence all around him, ready to take hold of him and punish him for even attempting such an exorcism. He had heard stories of priests being driven mad by the devils they had conjured up with their prayer book during such a service. He dared not look around, but stared, transfixed, at the groaning stone.

After a while the threat receded, and the day returned to him. The stone remained at an angle, but it was quiet. The birds were singing again, but he was completely alone. He could not imagine ever returning to the village. He had found the Squire to be an unreasonable man who had a grudge against the pure Church, and who knows what new charges he might concoct against him? His children had deserted him, and they had been his life. He had failed them. He hid his Bible and prayer book in the bag he had brought with him, removed every vestige of clothing that might show him to be a priest, and fled the place. He walked a long way until he reached a village where he knew he would not be recognised, giving himself out to be an itinerant beggar, and slept the night in a barn, as a beggar indeed was what he had become. He now possessed nothing but his prayers and his Bible.

After that day the Reverend Fallowfield was never seen again in Chapel Folding. Some said he had run away with the workmen when the stone began to groan, leaving the village for ever out of fear. Those that did not like him claimed he had gone to join the secret cult with Angel and her friends or had even been one of their number all along. Most, however, were of the opinion that something dreadful must have happened to him, although they could not say what, and were devastated at the news that he had vanished. Overall, the village was bereft. It was a terrible thing for them to have no spiritual guidance in their hour of greatest need. Had he known it, Squire Middleton had let his foolish vendetta deprive him of his greatest ally, the one man who could have held the village together and given them all hope.

Chapter Eleven

✦ ✦ ✦

The Courts of Justice

here was a curious phenomenon which Dr Grubb had read about in books, whereby the hair and fingernails of a dead person may continue to grow, even after they have left the body and departed this earth for the last time. It seemed to him that a similar phenomenon had overtaken the hand once owned by Peter Edmonton, which he now kept in a specimen jar in his study. Although it was certainly dead tissue, the fingernails continued to grow quite noticeably from day to day, and on the back of the hand there was a fresh growth of hair. The nails were now more than an inch long and had begun to curl around like claws. It also seemed to him that the hand had sometimes changed its position in the jar overnight and was facing a new way when he found it in the morning, as if it had moved by itself, although he told himself that this may have been an illusion. He decided that he would write a paper on the unusual growth of the dead hand, which he would present to the Royal Society in London. He thought perhaps it might bring him renown and lift him out of the obscurity of his life as a country doctor, but his hopes were suddenly dashed when one morning he found the specimen jar had broken. Embalming fluid was everywhere but the hand was nowhere to be seen. It appeared to have been spirited away during the night by person or persons unknown.

The City of London, where the Royal Society had its headquarters, was, in those days, an entirely new-built town. There was hardly a single building more than thirty years old, and most of its best-loved churches had not survived the Great Fire. Much of the town still remained unfinished. Only in hard-to-find corners, and down hidden lanes, were the vestiges of the old London still to be found, the odd building which had survived from the Middle Ages, the odd rough stony street bereft of smooth new cobbles. One such secret place was the Inner Temple, where Judge Nathan Mandeville had his rooms. The judges, lawyers and barristers had inherited their lodgings there from the Knights Templar, who had been tortured and murdered under orders from the Pope and the King of France more than three hundred years earlier. In the centre, and visible through the windows of his rooms, stood the slightly damaged round tower of the Temple Church, surrounded by the stone effigies of

Templar Knights ready to spring into action and defend Christianity when a ghostly trumpet sounded.

The talk in London in the time of Queen Anne was all about the coming of a new scientific age, the 'Enlightenment' as it came to be called. Under the continuing influence of such thinkers as René Descartes, Isaac Newton and John Locke, all human knowledge had been brought into the light of day, and arcane mysteries, dark alchemies and black magic were things of the past. This concept of enlightenment, and the age of reason, was very dear to the heart of Lord Justice Nathan Mandeville, although he did not believe that it would ever happen all on its own. In his youth he had been united with the fiery young Isobel Banham in his absolute hatred of Oliver Cromwell, the epitome of unreason, whose religiosity drove him to commit all sorts of atrocities in the name of God. Such mad extremism must never be allowed to take over again. Reason must reign supreme. But, unlike the fashionable Londoners, who were happily chattering away in their bright new coffee houses as if the enlightened age had already come, he knew that even within London foul crimes were being committed, and outside of London things were very different from what they imagined. If it were put to a vote of the whole country, the majority would still be of the opinion that the old devils, goblins and bogles were very much alive, and could any day come knocking at your door. The forces of darkness, in the form of false and superstitious beliefs, were, in his opinion, far too strong, and had to be forcibly rooted out. For this reason, he had not forgotten his recent visit to Chapel Folding. He knew that in the deep countryside there was a battle still to be fought, and Mandeville saw himself as a warrior, much as the Knights Templar had been.

The Judge was therefore very pleased, even delighted, when Peter Edmonton arrived at his chambers with a tale of woe, and only too happy to put aside the mundane business of the courts for what he believed to be more weighty matters.

Peter told him how he had run into difficulties on his journey. He had been stopped on the road by two men armed with staves. He told them that he came from Chapel Folding and was off to London on important business, but as soon as he mentioned the name of Chapel Folding, they would not let him pass.

'There's devilry in your village,' they said. 'We don't want your people crossing our land. Get you back the way you came!'

'It was like the plague years,' said Peter. 'They reacted as if I had some fatal infectious disease. And when they saw my missing hand, that really put the fear of God in them. "He's one of them!" they cried, and I had to beat them off with my whip and ride as fast as the demon from hell they thought I was just to get away.'

The Judge offered Peter a glass of Burgundy and asked him to explain in detail all that had happened in Chapel Folding since he'd left.

'I have not forgotten you,' he said. 'The village has been very much in my thoughts.'

'You wouldn't recognise it, sir,' said Peter. 'Dreadful things are now commonplace and mere children commit the foulest deeds.'

'Children?' said the Judge. 'What deeds?'

'Our maid Ellen had two young ones. Both are dead.'

'And how precisely did they die?'

'It seems that the other children killed them. There is some satanic ritual taking place up in the woods, connected with a young girl called Angel Blake. They meet near an old standing stone, the Currell Stone. I believe the Squire is making arrangements for the stone to be removed.'

'Unwise,' said the Judge.

'We fear that witchcraft has returned.'

'It is more than witchcraft.'

'We need your help, my lord.'

The Judge thought for a moment, as if weighing up the best way to proceed. Peter was anxious, lest the Judge should tell him to continue to play a waiting game. He had waited long enough.

'Things are moving so fast,' he said. 'I cannot say what may have happened since I left.'

'Well, I perceive the time is now ripe for my return,' said the Judge, cutting a slice from an apple and piercing it with his knife. 'I have made some researches, and I warn you, to destroy this evil, I will have to employ undreamed-of measures.'

The Judge had formed the opinion that to break the hold of superstitious fear, and the phantasms that it produced in the minds of men, it was necessary to introduce a greater and more tangible fear into their lives. One had to meet like with like, or all would be lost.

'If ever you are to become a judge, Peter,' he said as he ate the apple, 'you must learn to put all feeling and emotion aside. You must be prepared to sentence your own father to be hung, if he should deserve it.'

He led Peter down into a cellar beneath the buildings of the Inner and Middle Temple, where there was a collection of relics from the time of the Knights Templar. Only very few of the most senior members of the judiciary held a key to this cellar, and Peter knew it was a great privilege to be allowed to see what it contained.

'Some people like to imagine that what we have here, in this vault, is a superb collection of golden treasures, once robbed from the Temple in Jerusalem,' said the Judge, 'but you will find what is hidden here is far more practical. These are weapons of war.'

Peter looked around him at the rusting iron pikes, hooked knives, swords and proud old battered shields, remnants of one of the bloodiest times in world history, the Crusades. It felt as if the Knights Templar had left them behind hurriedly when disaster struck. In the centre of the room, laid out on a table specially made for the purpose, was a massive broadsword in the shape of a cross. The Judge explained that this weapon was called simply 'The Crusader's Sword', and that nobody knew what giant had owned it. The Judge suggested to Peter that he should try to pick it up, which Peter did, grasping it with his one hand and cautiously nestling it between his arms, but he could hardly move it more than an inch.

'It was thought by some that this sword must never have been used, because it was too heavy to wield, but I have proved them wrong. I have taught myself to lift it and to wield it. It is a matter of sheer hard work, and the most strenuous practice.'

The Judge grabbed the huge hilt of the sword in his two hands and began to prepare himself. Peter still believed he must be boasting, because it seemed impossible, but slowly, in his grasp, the whole sword began to rise from the table as if by magic. Peter would have thought it a miracle had he not seen the tremendous strain on the Judge's face and the blood vessels rising on his neck. He whirled it round in a huge circle, which caused Peter to back away in fear, and laid it down again.

'It is as sharp now,' said the Judge, 'as the day it was first ground. This sword was once thought to have magical powers, and according to some stories its two sharp edges sliced through the necks of many notorious unbelievers, including Al-Nasir himself,' but he added that such things were a complete lie, and of no interest to him. What did interest him was the effect it might have on the superstitious villagers of a little place like Chapel Folding.

He told Peter that, as a judge, he had a special task to uphold the truth at all costs.

'And what,' he said with a wicked smile, 'do you imagine "truth" to be?'

Peter suspected a trick.

'The bedrock,' he said, 'the one sure thing we can rely on?'

'Wrong,' snapped the Judge. 'The truth is what we believe it to be. That is why it is so important that we stamp out false beliefs!'

The Judge was not noted for his leniency, but when it suited him, he would spare the life of a criminal if he felt he might become a useful servant, with talents that should not be allowed to go to waste. Fairchild, the dumb strangler, the strength of whose arms was second to none, was given a second chance in this way, and Bridges, who had fed his victims to the pigs, had a way with animals, and was put in charge of the Judge's hunting dogs. In this manner he had built up an entourage of ex-criminals who had then become his bodyguards, and his soldiers, if called upon to fight.

Armed with the Crusader's Sword and with muskets and rifles distributed to his small private army, Judge Mandeville set off with Peter Edmonton to make his return visit to Chapel Folding. It was heavy going, the Judge's coach being weighed down and very slow. A little before they had reached their destination, Peter asked permission to leave the party and go off for a short while on his own. He was unable to go past the town of Sheffingham without paying a visit there to the local lunatic asylum, where he knew his beloved Rosalind was still imprisoned. The Judge was surprised and not best pleased by the request, but he recognised that Peter would be a useless soldier unless he was rid of that element of his past, and so he allowed it.

Peter rode off at speed. The Sheffingham Asylum was not far. Even if he found her languishing and in chains, Rosalind would know that she was not forgotten, and he would do everything he could to get her out of that dreadful place. When he arrived there, he found the fences were so high and the buildings so forbidding, their blank windowless walls stained with brown moss, that it seemed an impossible task even to gain entry. The gate into the building was at the back of it, where deliveries were made.

Peter presented himself well, and seeing that he was a gentleman, the guards became reasonably civil towards him. While keeping him firmly under observation, they led him through the wards of howling patients into the relatively civilised and well-appointed administrative quarters, and there, after a short wait, he was shown into the offices of the governor himself, who greeted him warmly. The governor had been a little disappointed when the guards told him that Peter was not one of the curious rich visitors who liked to come from time to time and view his lunatics. Friends and relatives of the inmates were rather less welcome, and they very rarely came, but he realised straight away that Peter was a gentleman and had money. Also, Peter was connected to a particular case that was of quite urgent interest to him, and he could perhaps cast some light upon a mystery.

He sat Peter down and told him that unfortunately he was too late. Another of the women in his care had taken against Rosalind Barton, and continually baited her, deliberately trying to make her angry, and although Rosalind had always kept herself to herself, saying very little, she could not be separated from her for ever. Only this last week that same young woman had been found dead in the asylum grounds, after being mauled by some wild beast, as it seemed from the deep scars and scratches that were on her.

Rosalind herself had disappeared that same night, having apparently climbed the asylum walls, a feat nobody would have thought possible, Rosalind being such a slight young thing. All attempts to find her in the surrounding countryside had been unsuccessful, and it was thought that she had fled the county. The governor regretted that Peter had had a wasted journey. He then gave Peter an old, scribbled note in which Rosalind had written, in surprisingly good English for a lunatic, that she felt she was possessed by a demon. Did Peter know something the governor did not know, and which could help them find her?

Peter sat in shock for a moment, then said he knew nothing, picked up his hat and was gone. He was full of a kind of desperate fury. What had happened? Where was she? Why had they allowed that other woman near her? He spurred his horse and rode on like the wind towards the only place where he thought and hoped she might have gone if her senses had returned to her, and that was Chapel Folding.

Chapter Twelve

✦ ✦ ✦

The Witch Hunts

eanwhile, in the village of Chapel Folding itself, fear was spreading. Groups of self-styled witch-hunters had sprung up, intent on revenge, but the objects of their fury, Angel Blake and her growing group of worshippers, had disappeared into the woods and were nowhere to be found.

Despite all the efforts of the Squire and his men to put a stop to witch-hunting, and to claim that the devil worshippers had been defeated and had left the area, they remained a constant presence in people's minds. Accusations of witchcraft were widespread. The village folk lived in fear that their children would suffer the same fate as Ellen Vespers' children, and stories of other missing, mutilated or murdered people were soon becoming commonplace. With the fear came the anger. When the Squire failed to bring things to order, bands of witch-hunters formed who were merciless to those that they suspected of having what they called the 'Devil's Skin'.

Not all the devil worshippers were without remorse. Rachel Downes, one of the two Downes sisters, who had once been a devout Christian, was plagued by nightmares after witnessing the murder of Cathy Vespers, in which her sister Margaret had played a part. She was torn in two between the overwhelming visceral attraction of the new-found cult and the agonising guilt which she felt at betraying the fundamental beliefs of Christianity. For other cult members there was no turning back, as they knew they would immediately be condemned to hell by the Church. Rachel, however, had one hope, and that was the leniency of the Reverend Fallowfield. She had heard that he had been freed from his wrongful imprisonment, and knew him to be a gentle man, perhaps capable of showing her a way out of the trap of sin into which she had fallen.

She went first to the rectory and found the place locked up. The windows were all dark and there was a heavy padlock on the door. It looked as if there had been no-one living there for some while. She walked around the building in despair. She felt the judgement of God had come upon her like a thunderbolt, and she could find no place of refuge. Hoping against hope, she ran to the church. She found it quite empty and bare, with none of the usual decoration that might have suggested a recent service. The Reverend Fallowfield was not there either. There was just one small woman in black, at prayer in a distant pew. This was Nell Swift, the mother of Dorcas Swift, praying for her vanished daughter. Rachel waited for her to rise and leave. They shared a half-smile as she passed. As soon as she had gone, Rachel herself went forward towards the altar. She fell on her knees, sobbing and begging God's forgiveness for what she had done, and the terrible scenes she had witnessed as a follower of Angel Blake. She chanted the Latin words '*miserere mei*' over and over.

But she was not yet alone. Nell Swift had not left the church. She had long suspected Rachel and her sister had defected from the true Church to join Angel Blake and her crowd of unbelievers, and what she now heard, hidden behind a pillar, confirmed her worst fears. She did not wait to hear the whole of Rachel's horrifying confession, but crept out so as not to disturb her, and climbed to the chamber from which the bells were rung.

After finishing her prayers, Rachel prostrated herself on the ground in front of the altar, and lay there for some while, when she heard a single bell tolling above her again and again. She could not imagine what this might mean. Surely it did not signify a church service. She rose. The sound of the bell seemed to ring all around her, growing ever louder, as if passing judgement on her. When she tried to leave the church, the significance of the bell became clear. A rabble had gathered outside, and they were out for her blood. Nell Swift had told them what she had said, and they needed no further evidence to condemn her. They carried her, screaming, and hung her from the nearest tree. Soon a search party was sent out to look for her sister, Margaret.

Within a couple of days of searching there was a hue and cry because Margaret had been seen down by the river, fetching water. An angry mob was hastily assembled, of which not only Nell Swift but also Angel's own father, Bill, was a member. He continued to maintain that his daughter was an innocent who had been seduced by others, and although there were few who believed him, they were glad to employ his help in hunting for witches. He was good at it, and unremitting in his efforts. They were all united in fury as they formed a ring around the unsuspecting Margaret, and closed in for the kill. Because her big dress made swimming all but impossible, Margaret had nowhere to turn.

Ralph Gower heard the commotion and came running up, the others urging him to join in the hunt, but he held back because he had suffered too much from mindless violence already.

'I have her,' came the cry.

Ralph could see that they had already caught their prey, and despite her terrified screams to let her go, two strong men had hold of her. One held her up by her legs and the other was about to beat her with a stave. He yelled at them not to kill a young woman who, for all they knew, might be completely innocent. Reluctantly, but because Ralph now had some respect within the village, they paused in their savage beating, and took counsel among themselves.

A compromise was reached, and Margaret was dropped to the ground. It was proposed that having caught her they would 'swim' her, to see if she was a witch. The location, where the lazy river formed itself into a deep, silent pool, was perfect for such a judgement to take place. It was a common belief among simple folk that if thrown into a river a witch would always be able to save herself, as the devil would keep her afloat, whereas an innocent woman would go under. Ralph may have not been gifted with huge intelligence, but he saw the fallacy in that argument.

'If she should float then she be a witch,' they cried.

'And if she drowns, you done a murder,' countered Ralph, and interposed himself between the struggling Margaret and the water. Margaret bit one of her assailants.

'She's one of them alright!' they snarled.

Ralph continued to defend her, but there were too many of them against him, and he was pulled back. Their anger was such that they did not really care if Margaret Downes was innocent or not. Someone had to suffer, to slake their thirst for revenge. Margaret was hurled into the river, and as might have been expected, the weight of her waterlogged clothes soon pulled her beneath the surface, however hard she tried to swim. They watched until she disappeared, and the last bubble no longer told them where she was, and then they began to disperse, feeling that some sort of justice had been done, however unsatisfactory it might be.

As soon as he was released, Ralph rushed into the water and felt around in the murky depths for their victim, who was not too difficult to find. He used all his strength to drag her out and, streaming with water, he dropped her on the bank. She lay motionless for quite a while, but then she spluttered a little, and choked. It was not much breath that came from her, but it was enough to show that she was still alive. Dark river water dribbled from her mouth. As he carried her senseless body back to the farm, it occurred to Ralph more than once how blessed it would have been if he had been able to save Cathy in the same way.

A similar thought occurred to Ellen when he arrived in the farm kitchen.

'I thought for a moment thou were bringing my Cathy back to me,' she said.

'They threw her in the river, and she sank straight away, and none would pull her out. They gave her up for dead, but she'm still breathing.'

Ralph and Ellen sat Margaret in a big wooden chair, close to the fire.

'The poor lass. What have they been doing to her?'

'Chased her for miles, I reckon,' said Ralph. 'Thought her was a devil worshipper.'

'Oh glory, and is she, then?' said Ellen with alarm.

'They suspect anyone. There were people I knew there, people I used to call my friends, all for drowning her.'

Ellen looked at Margaret, unconscious and helpless. She was a fine young woman with long, curling hair and stretched out on her chair she could not have looked less like a witch, but she had many bruises after what had happened to her. Ellen could see she had been badly maltreated.

'She shall have Cathy's bed,' she said. 'Ralph, can you fetch it down?'

While Ralph was away fetching the bed, Ellen began to relieve Margaret of her soaking clothes, and sponge away the slime from her face and arms, being careful not to hurt the places where there were scratches and bruises under the mud. She was about to pull away her underskirts when she found they were stuck to the side of her thigh. She feared that there was some sort of festering sore there and let out a cry when she discovered a patch of wet and muddy hair. The look of it terrified her.

'Ralph! Ralph! Help!' she called.

Ralph dropped the bed and ran to the kitchen door. Ellen was wiping the mud away, but there was a large patch of fur beneath it, growing on Margaret's thigh.

'What is it, Ralph?' she said.

Ralph remained in the doorway.

'I prayed I'd never see that again,' he said. 'That's what they call the Devil's Skin.'

Despite this grim discovery, they decided they could not desert poor Margaret, as many others might have done, but treated her as if she had fallen victim to some dreadful, and possibly contagious, illness. Ralph ran to get help from Dr Grubb.

The doctor gave one look at her leg and was appalled.

'Let her die, say I,' was his reaction.

'But why, sir?' said Ralph.

'That on her thigh is the mark of the devil. Little wonder the villagers wanted rid of her.'

At first the doctor had regarded the 'Devil's Skin' as some kind of natural epidemic, but the more he saw of it and knew about it, the more his medical education deserted him, and the old fears of black magic, which he had known from his childhood, had begun to return.

'We would like to save her for Cathy's sake,' said Ellen, 'but we have not the skill.'

'Is there nothing you can do?' said Ralph. 'Could you not cut it out?'

'To what end? Most like the skin would grow again. Besides, the operation would be most delicate, and I am no surgeon.'

'But I have heard your surgery is a wonder, doctor.'

'You stitched up Mister Peter's arm real well,' put in Ellen.

'Are you out of your senses?' insisted the doctor. 'What if people found out?'

'Please, sir, out of charity,' said Ralph, and then added wisely, 'and if you were to save her, that'd be som'ert what no-one else could do.'

This appeal to Dr Grubb's vanity began to win him round, and he asked for Margaret to be lifted on to the kitchen table where he could look better at the fur, and consider performing an operation, so long as nobody was told that he had attempted such a thing. Otherwise, it would be more than his life was worth.

'I hope you're right, Ralph, and we shall not waste our pains,' he said. 'Hold her fast if she wakes.'

Ellen poured some salt into a bowl and began to look for bandages. The doctor thought it prudent that some of these be used to tie the patient to the table.

'Have you the eau de vie?' he asked. Ellen fetched it.

The doctor took a small scalpel from his bag and began to cut. Neither Ellen nor Ralph liked to look at what was happening, and Margaret began to stir from her stupor, making the doctor's work more difficult. Ralph held her down, as under the scalpel the skin began to come away. The doctor was careful, and made a clean wound with very little blood. All the same Margaret suddenly awoke and began to scream.

'Quiet her!' said the doctor, fearing that someone, somewhere, might hear what was going on. Ralph held his hand over her mouth. The doctor continued his work, although she struggled, as if he was separating a deadly parasite from her body. Despite her twists and turns, he soon held up a large area of cut skin. It was covered in fur, and for a moment it moved, then lay limp in his hand. Her leg, though badly scarred, was free. It seemed to all three of them that a good job had been done, and Margaret might yet enjoy a life free of her curse.

'There,' said the doctor, as he curled the skin into a jar, 'not so bad.'

'The Lord be praised,' said Ellen.

'But we must burn that skin,' said Ralph, 'destroy it good and proper.'

'Yes, yes,' said the doctor, although he did not pay much attention to what Ralph was saying. He had never performed such an operation before and was amazed at his success. Ellen examined the wound.

'Well, look at that,' she said. 'There's no blood.'

'Did you see that, doctor?' said Ralph.

'I was aware,' said the doctor, with a smile.

'Shall I live?' asked Margaret, drowsily.

'Of course thou shall,' said Ellen.

Margaret stretched out her arm towards the doctor, who backed away anxiously and hid from her the jar which contained the skin. As soon as he could, he sneaked out of the room, holding his new trophy inside his coat, as if afraid it might escape from him and some-how rejoin its owner.

'What is your name, child?' asked Ellen, when the doctor had gone.

'Margaret. I'm the devil's child,' was the response.

'Hush, thou'rt our child now,' said Ellen, hoping to coax Margaret out of her nightmare.

'I must go to my Master,' said Margaret, still in a kind of delirium. 'Why do my leg pain me so?'

'There was a growth,' said Ralph, 'but the doctor cut it all away.'

'You lie,' said Margaret, now more determined and awake, looking Ralph straight in the eye. 'You have cut away my skin!' She struggled to get up but failed. She was still bound to the table. Ellen gave her some eau de vie, but she spat it out. All at once she began weeping like a little child.

'There,' said Ellen, 'the Lord have mercy on thee, and bring thee soon to health.' Hopeful that her tears meant that she might yet recover from her fantasies, Ellen and Ralph decided to loosen her bonds and leave her alone to sleep.

It was a forlorn hope as it turned out, but it gave them both a task in life. They carried her, sleeping, into the living room, and laid her on Cathy's bed. In the morning Ralph came with a large bunch of flowers and herbs which he had picked for her, thinking that the fresh scent of them might help with her cure.

'Thou be safe now,' he said. 'Ellen will take good care of thee. Thou'rt a lucky lass, to be sure.'

Margaret was sitting on a chair, wearing the dry clothes which Ellen had prepared for her, with her leg raised on a stool, and looking out of the window.

'You can't keep me here,' she said. 'I shall run away. Angel wants me.'

'Now listen here, Margaret,' said Ralph, becoming angry. 'Angel herself has run away. She has disappeared and deserted you. You do not serve her anymore!'

At this moment Ellen came in with a bowl of warm fruit and oats. Margaret turned to her while pointing at Ralph.

'He stole my master's skin. He shall pay with his, and thou with thine!' she snarled.

'You leave off your threats, young madam,' said Ellen, 'or the Good Lord will strike thee down afore thou know it!'

'My lord will strike you down,' retorted Margaret. 'He has true servants! All of us give our flesh that he shall have a body, and live again!'

'You need to learn some gratitude, young lady!' said Ellen, thrusting the bowl on to the table in front of her and hurrying out again, close to tears.

Margaret turned away from Ellen, and grasped Ralph's hand in both of hers, looking hard into him.

'Thou knows our Master,' she said. 'It were thou what showed us the way when thou dug him out and gave him life. Come thou and serve him. Thou shall give some piece of thyself, and Angel will bless thee. Thou shall lie with Angel. Thou shall lie with me!'

With that she stretched her hands further up his arm, coiling her fingers round it. For a while Ralph stood mesmerised, hardly able to believe what he was hearing. Margaret began to draw him towards her. Enveloped in her dark aura, he could almost have embraced her, had he not heard Dr Grubb's bony nag in the yard outside.

'Ellen!' he called. 'Come thou, the doctor's here!' He pulled away his hand from Margaret and snapped at her, 'Why did I think thou could be saved?'

With one last furious glance in her direction, he left the room to go and meet the doctor. Margaret fell back into her chair with a strange look of ecstasy in her eyes.

'Good day, Ralph,' said the doctor cheerily, as Ralph came out into the yard, exhausted, and slumped down on a mound of hay. 'How is it with our patient?'

Ralph held his head in his hands. He shook it.

'Oh, sir, I am mistaken. 'Tis a hopeless case. She speaks of nothing but her master the devil.'

The doctor's mood immediately changed. All his fears returned.

'Then I was right to think no good would come of it. The news I get from the village is grave too. Every day someone is missed. Some claimed to have met the devil on the road, hobbling on one leg, they say. He's getting closer, I tell you. Everyone is suspected of having the skin. I just hope they don't get wind of what I did for that girl of yours.' He gave an anxious glance towards the farmhouse where he knew the 'girl' was still hiding.

Ellen knew better than to make any further attempt to argue with Margaret, as that only led to anger. Her one hope was to prove to her that she was loved, by accepting her, and then to win her round. Ellen was not only a good cook; she firmly believed that all the world's ills could be cured with the right food, and she was as happy preparing quail and chestnuts for a gentleman such as the Judge as she was when making a simple posset to cure a cold. She noticed sadly that Margaret still had not touched her warm oats.

'Why won't thou eat?' she said. 'Thou'rt all bone, thou be so thin.'

'I want no charity,' said Margaret.

'Why wilt thou not accept the help of those as want to care for thee? We do it out of love for thee.'

'My Master, who you call the devil, he will care for me. He has walked in our woodlands here since the earliest of days. He is the great Beast, the Behemoth, whose footsteps thunder in the night. The Christians thought they could cut him in a thousand pieces and build their churches on his grave. But he is strong, and each day he grows stronger, as we give part of ourselves to him. You will not be able to resist him for much longer. He is everywhere!'

'Come, thou stubborn young hussy!' said Ellen, allowing her anger and frustration to show again.

'Hussy yourself! I'll bide no longer!' and with a great effort Margaret rose from her chair and lunged her whole body at Ellen. Ellen was caught off guard, and fell over backwards, while Margaret took her chance and hobbled out of the door. Ellen was winded and slow to get to her feet, and by the time she did so, Margaret was nowhere to be seen. She looked this way and that in different rooms, and eventually concluded that Margaret must have already left the house. She ran out into the yard, where the doctor and Ralph were still talking.

'Ralph, have you seen Margaret?'

'No.'

'We've seen no-one,' added the doctor, with alarm.

'Margaret!'

'She can't be far, not with that leg.'

'She'm vanished.'

'Margaret!'

'The poor child. She'll be killed for certain if they find her,' said Ellen as she searched.

'And then we won't be safe either, none of us,' added the doctor. 'She will tell about her leg, and what I've done, tell it to her godless clan, and they'll come and punish me.'

This general panic seemed to have infected the animals in the farmyard. Soon a whole herd of cattle headed towards the farm. Behind them was a horseman on a white horse, riding in at the gate. The doctor was terrified and did not like to look.

'Are they coming for us?' he asked, not sure in his fear who 'they' might be.

'It's the master!' called Ralph, full of excitement. Peter Edmonton rode into the yard. With his arrival Margaret was, for a while, forgotten.

'How goes it?' he called out.

'This place is in a terrible bad way, master,' said Ralph. 'You cannot imagine. It's all gone mad!'

'In what way mad?'

'Everyone goes in fear of everyone else. They're out hunting for witches.'

'There was one here,' added the doctor.

'Well, I bring good news,' said Peter, as he descended from his horse. 'Help is on its way. I met Judge Mandeville in London, and after I had talked to him and told him of our troubles, he decided to return, and he brings men with him.'

'Thank the Lord,' said the doctor.

'He was already prepared for this moment, and he knows what is needed.'

'The Squire must be informed,' said Ralph.

'I must have overtaken the Judge and his men on the way,' added Peter. 'I went a different route. Ralph, could you take the horse? I'm famished. Ellen, I need supper.'

And for a moment it seemed as if normality had returned, a little oasis of calm in the middle of a storm. The doctor rode off to find the Squire.

Chapter Thirteen

✦ ✦ ✦

The Ultimate Sacrifice

t was growing dark by the time the lanterns of the Judge's coach could be seen approaching Chapel Folding through the woods. It had been a hard journey for the heavy coach, as the road was deep in mire, and the spokes of one of the wheels had to be repaired on the way. Large crates were loaded on top of the coach behind the silent coachman, and behind the coach there were outriders on dark horses. The Judge was not in a good mood, but he had a look of brooding determination, as of someone who had a harsh task to perform and must not falter in the performing of it.

As the coach reached the Banham farm, a small group of people had gathered to meet it, including Squire Middleton, who bowed deeply. The Judge had little time for words of welcome, and when the Squire told him of his failed attempt to unearth the Currell Stone, he did little to disguise his rage. In his eyes, that was the most stupid thing the Squire had yet done. He snapped at him that it could ruin everything. If it was to be destroyed in its entirety, the cult must have its central meeting place intact. The worshippers must be allowed to gather there, knowing nothing of his arrival, which was why he had chosen to come under cover of darkness. Everything must be done in secret. The Squire then bade him good night and arranged to meet with him in the morning.

The crates, which seemed to contain growling livestock, were removed from the coach's roof. The horses, along with the coach itself and various other smaller crates, were given a home in the stables, while the Judge avoided the servants who had come to meet him and, accompanied by Peter, went straight into the farmhouse. Once inside he felt more able to relax, with faces that he knew.

'I never thought to see you again, my lord,' confessed Ellen with a curtsey. Ralph echoed the general belief that the devil was now alive in the village and the Judge was the only person who might save them.

'I arrive country fashion,' said the Judge, 'and I wish to be brief. I understand this village is diseased. Tell me precisely, what are the symptoms?'

Ellen was the first to speak.

'Oh, sir, my poor children both have gone, and countless others maybe. They give their bodies to the devil.'

'Many people have lost limbs,' explained Peter, 'in the belief that they are helping the devil to grow.'

The Judge listened intently to everything they said.

'I am grieved that you have to suffer so, but now at last we begin to see the true nature of the evil.'

'There is an epidemic of some strange new disease which produces a fur which grows upon the skin,' put in the doctor, who had followed the others inside. 'I have a sample with me.'

'We found a young woman as worshipped the devil,' said Ralph. 'They were all for killing her, but she survived. Her name is Margaret. She bore the devil's skin.'

'And where is this woman? This devil worshipper?'

'She escaped, my lord,' said Ellen, 'more's the pity.'

'Well, Ralph Gower, again you are giving me nothing but stories, without any evidence. A woman who has vanished is worth nothing.'

'I believe I have something, my lord,' said the doctor. 'This was her skin.'

He fished out his glass jar with Margaret's furred skin curled inside it. The Judge took it and held it to the light, considering it for a short while. He put his hand into the jar and pulled out the skin. He then ran it through his fingers and sniffed it.

'This will be sufficient,' he said.

Without another word, the Judge gestured upwards and was conducted to his room, where he prepared himself for sleep. The hunt would begin in the morning.

There was much whispering among the inhabitants of the farm as to what form his plans might take. No-one had dared to ask.

The Judge was up at first light, and ordered his crates to be opened, and his dogs to be unchained. They were massive beasts, four of them, barking loudly at their first taste of freedom. The Judge began to feed them with strips of dried meat, paying particular attention to the big black dog, which was his favourite. Ralph came to see what was happening, and the Judge answered his un-spoken question without bothering to turn round.

'I mean to run this devil of yours to earth. These dogs are ravenous, and they know how to tear the devil's heels.'

He took the jar containing Margaret's skin, offering it for each of the dogs to take a sniff. They growled angrily at the smell of it. Peter came out of the farm at this moment, and saw the dogs being given the scent.

'Not everyone who has the devil's skin worships him,' he warned. 'Some of them are innocent victims, but they may smell the same.'

'Leave me to judge whom I consider innocent,' snapped the Judge, and motioned his dog handlers to allow the dogs to find and follow Margaret's trail, which they did with alacrity. The handlers could barely restrain them.

Margaret, in her new-found freedom, had regained much of her strength, and was running fast. Periodically she would stop and give out her special bird cry, waiting for a response. She and her friends had practised these cries until they could barely be distinguished from the birds themselves, although they were easily recognised by each other. Since the attack on the Currell Stone by the Squire's men, Angel had arranged alternative meeting places dotted among the woods and hills, and Margaret ran from one to another, hoping to hear an answering call. On the previous night she had failed to hear any, and when darkness fell, she had spent the night in fear and confusion. Did they know of her shame, she wondered, that her skin had been cruelly cut from her? Would she no longer be accepted? Had her Master rejected her? But in the morning hope had returned. She knew that her Master was nearly complete. His presence was so great that it permeated the entire woodland. His ghost was alive in every tree. When he was fully manifest, she knew that she had nothing to fear. His power would protect her, and all who served him. When he was whole, he would be so great that no-one would dare come near him, nor enter the woods that were his kingdom.

Then she heard the dogs for the first time. Even though they were still in the distance, she knew they were coming for her. Like a fox, she deliberately ran through streams and along their banks, trying to disguise her scent. Then, just as she began to give up hope of avoiding the dogs, she heard a bird call. It could mean safety, but she did not yet know from whence it came. She must find that place before the dogs found her. She heard the call again. At last, she located it. It came from the old chalk pit, somewhere that they had already used for rituals, somewhere she knew well. She gave out her own special bird cry, and it was answered. She still could not see precisely where the answering call came from, but she knew it was nearby. The dogs were circling round.

'It's me, Margaret!' she called out loud. 'I've come back . . . Angel!'

'Who calls Angel?'

A figure appeared above her, so completely clothed in white that it almost vanished into the white chalk cliff. It was Angel herself.

'Is it to be tonight?' asked Margaret.

'It is! And art thou ready, Margaret?' said Angel.

'Help me, Angel,' begged Margaret.

'Why should I help thee, Margaret?'

'Save me, Angel, the dogs are after me!'

'What dogs are those? What hast thou done, Margaret?'

'Nothing. They tried to drown me, and I escaped, but I'm afeard. Let me come with thee!'

'Yes, Margaret. Come to me!' said Angel, holding out her arms. Margaret struggled towards Angel, and Angel encouraged her to come closer. There was a snap, and an iron beast, worse than a dog, had her by the ankle. A man-trap dug its teeth into her leg.

'Thou tell-tale bitch, thou set the dogs on me,' said Angel.

'Course I didn't! Get me out of this!' panicked Margaret.

Angel did not answer but took pleasure in the fact that she now had Margaret totally in her power.

'I hear the dogs. Whose are they?'

'I don't know where they're from,' Margaret pleaded. 'They've been chasing me for miles.'

'And who set them on thee?'

Margaret struggled with her answer.

'Could be they were sent from the farm.'

'The farm?'

'Mistress Banham's farm. They kept me prisoner best part of a week.'

'What did you tell them, Margaret?'

'Nothing. I said nothing.'

'And they just kept you prisoner, and did nothing?' Angel was beginning to strongly suspect that she had not yet heard the whole story.

'Yes! Let me out!' moaned Margaret. She made a violent attempt to break free of Angel's man-trap but fell headlong.

'Art thou ready to give up thy skin tonight?' said Angel, drawing Margaret's skirt upwards. Margaret tried to prevent her from doing so, but Angel persisted.

'Art thou ready?'

Angel looked at the clean scar on Margaret's thigh, her worst suspicions confirmed.

'They did it to me,' whimpered Margaret. 'There was nothing I could do. They took it from me. Save me, Angel!'

Angel looked at Margaret with complete contempt.

'Thou bain't worth saving, Margaret. Let the dogs eat thee!'

Angel ran off, leaving Margaret unable to move. Soon she became a flicker of chalk-white moving among the thorn bushes, then she was gone. As Margaret watched her go, the vision of Ralph with his bunch of flowers strangely came into her mind. Despite her obsession to escape it, that farm had introduced a brief moment of peace into her life. But then she was aware that the dogs would soon be upon her.

The Judge and his dog handlers had heard Margaret's cries for help, and knew their quarry was not far off. Then as the white cliff of the chalk pit came into view, they had a sighting. The Judge ordered them to bring the dogs to heel, so as not to lose the element of surprise, but as they crept closer it grew more and more apparent that for some reason the young woman was not moving or could not move. Then, unexpectedly, one of the dogs broke free and leapt ahead, dragging its chain and barking furiously, forcing its handler to run after it. Seeing it approach, Margaret tried to drag the heavy man-trap with her in an attempt to climb a tree, but it was too firmly staked into the ground. The black dog leapt upon her, biting at her, and it was making for her throat, when its handler, the pig farmer, just caught it in time. He held it back, with its muzzle snarling inches from her face. The other dogs soon joined it, followed by the Judge, with Ralph behind him.

'Is this the one?' asked the Judge.

'It is, your worship,' said Ralph, although it hurt him to see her so helpless, and in such a state. He set about pulling the jaws of the man-trap apart, but it was far too hard for one man to do.

'What is your name, woman?' snapped the Judge.

'Margaret.'

'Who set traps for thee?'

'Get it off me,' begged Margaret, although she would not give him a name. The Judge signalled to the dumb strangler, who took over the task from Ralph, opening the trap as if it were a child's toy.

Once free, Margaret turned on Ralph.

'Pig!' she yelled. 'Why didst thou set the dogs on me?'

'Come with me,' said the Judge, grabbing her arm in a vice-like grip, 'and I shall tell thee why.'

Not far off was a small old disused barn, deserted and stooped with the years, and the Judge selected it as a suitable place for his interrogation. Margaret was dragged inside, limping.

'Bind her!' said the Judge, and she was tied with a rope firmly to a beam, so that her feet barely touched the ground. The dogs, who were angry at losing the opportunity of mauling their prey, still followed her with their eyes, growling.

'You may leave us now, Ralph,' said the Judge, seeing Ralph still standing awkwardly at the entrance. His sympathetic attitude towards Margaret might prove a liability when the Judge did what had to be done. Ralph was reluctant to leave the woman whose life he had once saved, but he sadly turned away. When she saw him go, Margaret lost all her anger towards him. She called after him, begging him to turn back, as he seemed like her only hope.

'Be silent!' said the Judge, as he unsheathed a thin rapier from within his gnarled walking stick. He toyed with her dress, running the point of the rapier down her body. The threat was always there, but his tone became more restrained, as if in a court of law.

'I do not wish to hurt thee more than is necessary,' he said, 'but I have to ascertain certain facts.'

'I don't know what you mean,' Margaret said sulkily, turning her head away. The Judge turned her head back, with the rapier held below her chin. His tone remained calm, but she could clearly feel that beneath his superficial precision there was a fierce anger which at any moment might erupt, and she was very afraid of it.

'It is my intention utterly to destroy every one of your evil practices,' he said. 'No consideration will prevent me. I will stop at nothing, so . . .' and here he left a pause before snarling, 'speak!'

The dogs picked up on his words and began to bark loudly. They were tethered to a low beam, but not so far away as to present no threat. Despite this, Margaret remained defiant.

'Never!'

The Judge's face clouded over, as if he had not expected such a determined response. He made a small incision close to her ear, so that she could feel the blood trickling down her throat.

'That is not the answer I wished for. It will go better for you if you confess.' He pressed the point of his rapier against her windpipe.

'I didn't kill no-one,' she gasped.

'Perhaps you did not, perhaps you did, and certainly you were there,' said the Judge. 'Perhaps you were deluded or held against your will, but who will know when you are swinging from the gibbet?' He withdrew the rapier enough to allow her to speak clearly.

'Tell me! Where is Angel Blake!' he bellowed. Again, the dogs joined him to reinforce his message. Margaret looked away, but the mention of Angel's name made her very much aware that had it not been for Angel's betrayal, she would not now be facing almost certain death. Her fury at Angel, the one person whom she had trusted above all others, welled up inside her until finally she spat it out.

'Bitch! She was in the woods just now.'

'You saw her in the woods?'

'She's the one that trapped me, almost cut my leg in two. It was her killed Cathy and Mark and the others.'

Now that he could feel he had the beginning of a confession, the Judge put away his rapier and moved closer. Once unleashed, Margaret's rage at Angel was unrelenting.

'Let her hang, my lord, let her hang!'

'If Angel is still in these parts,' said the Judge, 'where then do you meet her?'

'Anywheres,' was Margaret's unsatisfactory response.

'Where is your meeting place?' repeated the Judge, now threatening her with the clubbed end of his stick. Margaret spluttered.

'Anywhere ... anywhere that's hidden,' she said, but seeing that this answer could easily cost her a blow of the stick, she added more.

'There's to be a final meeting tonight.'

'Tonight?'

'No, 'twas last night ... 'tis passed!' Margaret suddenly realised she had said too much but could not lie her way out of it.

'Tonight? Where?'

'In the clearing ... by the chapel ... where that old druid stone is leaning. Our Master will take his final form tonight! Our last victim is to sacrifice his limb! Everyone will come! Tim Parsons will be there, and Will Courtenay. Mistress Banham will be there.'

'Mistress Banham?' The Judge frowned deeply.

'Yes, sir, and Mistress Barton is with us now, and Winsome Rogers, and Dorcas Swift.' Once she had begun, she couldn't stop, reeling out a whole long list of names which seemed to include most people in the village, alive or dead, until the Judge had to call a halt to it. He was still not sure whether she was always telling the truth, but she had told enough.

'This is all I need to know,' he said.

He then turned away. One of the handlers struck her across the face and left her hanging. In desperation she continued to be defiant, shouting after them as they walked away.

'It won't do you no good,' she yelled. 'Tonight my Master will be complete. He'll be too powerful for you. He'll destroy you. You're too late. You don't have a hope!'

But when they had gone, she was faced with the reality that it was she who didn't have a hope, hanging where she was, tied to a post. She could expect no mercy if she fell into the hands of either party. Someone had to find her soon if she were to survive, but people rarely gave this old barn a second thought, and if they did, and found her there, what might they do to her?

Ralph Gower had a method of coping with the tragedies of life, which was always to continue with simple work until the pain lessened. He was untiring, like a cart-horse, and he would keep the world going when all the others fell by the wayside. Even when Cathy died and the sunlight went out of his life, he put all his effort into the Banham farm, and kept it alive. Though a mere servant, he had provided the example by which Peter Edmonton could rebuild his life. He had helped the Judge in his efforts to suppress evil in the village, even though he himself could not fully comprehend the nature of that evil.

But even carthorses cannot go on for ever, and Ralph had noticed that ever since that day when he had ploughed up the creature in Tarrant's Field, the menial tasks which had been the salt of his life became harder to perform, as if the energy were being drawn out of him. At first, he kept going as he always did, but more recently he had found that it was progressively harder and he was becoming clumsy. It was not so easy for him to find refuge in his work.

After he had left the Judge and Margaret in the barn, feeling that there was nothing else he could do, he went to cut hay in an old meadow to provide fodder for the horses. He was tired. Very soon he noticed that the ground beneath his feet began to feel more uneven, and that he was sweating more than usual as he wielded his sickle. A number of crows and gulls began to circle round him as he worked, just as they had done on the fateful day when his troubles all started. They seemed to be watching him from the nearby trees, as if waiting for another catastrophe.

Then he did something which he would never usually have done. He wielded the sickle so carelessly that he cut his own ankle, as if he were an inexperienced young apprentice, not a tried-and-tested workman. It was all part of the clumsiness from which he had recently been suffering. He hoped the cut was not too deep, and he began to unravel the thick sock which had fortunately protected him. It was then he saw something which shocked him to his core. The whole of his ankle inside his sock was covered in fur. He recognised it at once as the same as he had seen growing on Margaret. It was the 'Devil's Skin'. He too was infected with it. He remembered how, following the ploughing, he had developed an itch on his right ankle, but he had thought nothing of it. He had put his foot accidentally into a hole in the field, and probably scratched himself. He never imagined that his sore ankle would later erupt in such a way. Beneath the fur, within his ankle, something appeared to be moving. He almost vomited when he saw it.

What should he do? All that he could now think was that he must hide his affliction from the world. The Judge must never see it, nor Mister Peter, nor Ellen, and even more importantly it must not be spotted by any of Angel's followers. Even if it should get worse, and hurt him terribly, the world must never know. His ankle did now hurt, not only because of the cut, but on no account must he stagger, or be seen to be limping. He bound his wound in a handkerchief and pulled the sock and breeches over the fur. In doing so, he discovered the extent of it was much greater than he had first imagined. It was creeping up his leg. He could not bear to look at it.

He went straight to his mother's lodging to be sure that she was provided with all she needed, if he had to go away for a long time. She could see the anxiety on his face, but he told her it was nothing, that he had hurt himself accidentally. That was all. He gave her a kiss on the forehead, and as he did so, the thought entered his head that this might be the last time. He might never see her again. He tried to hide his distress from his mother with a smile, and she smiled back unsuspectingly, as he set off for the Banham farm.

Ralph had never thought that he was cut out to be a hero. He had failed badly when it came to protecting his beloved Cathy, so how could he hope to save a whole village, but that was what he, poor simple Ralph, was being called upon to do. He had been the first to uncover the eye of the devil, and now the worshippers would be after him, to make the devil whole. That was something which he must prevent at all costs. He told himself that he must not arrive late at the farm, or do anything unusual, or people might suspect that something had happened, but he could not hide it from himself that this was no ordinary day. It seemed as if the forest itself were watching him.

Then came another familiar, if uncomfortable, sound: the barking of the Judge's dogs, at first far off, but then drawing closer. He wondered who they were searching for now, and slowly it dawned on him, as the barking grew louder and louder, that it was him they were pursuing.

It was quite possible that they had already picked up the scent of the Devil's Skin that was on him. He could not easily run away, as his bad leg would make his progress impossibly slow. He decided to continue, limping while pretending not to limp, towards the doubtful safety of the farm.

He knocked repeatedly on the kitchen door until Ellen let him in. He looked exhausted, but it wasn't just ordinary weariness, she could tell. He was sick.

'What's wrong with thy leg?' she asked.

'Nothing,' he replied, sitting down on the nearest wooden chair, and stretching it away from him. Ellen tried to take a closer look at it.

'Don't touch it,' he said. 'Art thou by thyself?'

He was wondering if he could be overheard, and if he could confide in Ellen, she being the one person in the world with whom he felt halfway safe.

'Yes,' she said, frowning.

'There's no-one else?'

'No. Why dost'ou keep asking?'

'Where's Mister Peter?'

'I thought you knew. He's down the village with the rest of them, the Squire and all. Has thou not heard? The Judge be causing a great purge. Half the village is up in arms. Thou should be there. Thou'll be missed.'

This came as something of a surprise to Ralph. Things had progressed further than he had thought. The Judge had a particular objective in mind and was raising an army.

'Will they be coming back here, do you think?'

'Maybe. I imagine so.'

'I mustn't be here when they come.'

'Why? What has thou done?'

'I done naught, but I fear they are after me.'

'If there is som'ert, the Judge ought to know.'

Ralph reacted with terror at the thought.

'No. No, he mustn't! As thou loved Cathy, don't breathe a word to anyone that thou saw me. I have to hide.'

Ellen was more and more bewildered. She could not think what was wrong with him.

Ralph's mind was working fast. If he went back into the woods, he would be found by Angel and her clan. They would want the skin from off his leg to make their god 'complete', as they called it. He must not go there. But if he tried to hide in the farm, the Judge and his dogs would sniff him out easily, and 'purge' him, as Ellen said. There was no room in the whole house where he would not be found . . . except perhaps one.

'No-one ever goes to the spare room now?' said Ralph.

'You stay down here. That room is the last place thou ought to go.'

'But no-one has gone in there since Mister Peter, and they won't now, not even the dogs,' and before Ellen could stop him, he was clambering up the stairs and into the unknown. She stayed where she was. She would defend him with her life if anyone came looking, but she was not about to climb those stairs. Ralph grabbed a hammer to prise open the nails in the door.

He was right to go and hide, because almost immediately after he had gone up to the loft, Peter arrived home, followed by the Judge and a handful of his men. They were searching the farm for any weapons they could find and discussing their plan of attack. Ralph tried to listen to them from above. He was too far off to hear much of what they said, but once in a while voices spoke loudly, and he picked up certain things. There was to be some sort of battle in the woods that night. A great atmosphere of urgency prevailed; tonight, the last victim would give his skin to the devil, and the village folk believed the devil would 'take his form', whatever form that might be. Ralph was mostly confused by this talk, but of one thing he felt more and more certain. He himself was the 'last victim' of whom they spoke. He had the skin, and the devil worshippers would certainly come to take it from him.

Peter and the Judge returned to the village without ever searching the attic. It never entered their minds to do so. On the village green, they joined Squire Middleton, who was assembling his collection of volunteers to fight alongside the Judge's men in the forthcoming raid. Those that could charge and fire a weapon were supplied with a musket or rifle, irrespective of how accurate their aim might be. Those that could not handle guns were given more homely weapons – a pike, a pitchfork, a scythe, and the like – and some of them carried a rough weapon they had made themselves. Even old Ned Carter had been coerced into joining them and had been armed with a pitchfork and a wooden torch. Everyone was needed, as so many villagers had now defected to the other side. The Squire had brought with him a large barrel of beer to boost their confidence, and they all drank from it copiously.

'What ye as Christians call Satan and the Devil,' said the Judge, 'these worshippers call their Master, and an ancient god from pagan times. This is the nature of their delusion, but a delusion it remains! We are fighting a Satan of the mind!'

There were stories circulating about the enormous strength and supernatural power of their common enemy, and both the Judge and the Squire felt it imperative to put an end to these tales, as under no circumstances could they take on an army who were half-prepared to run away. This was a serious matter and must be treated in a disciplined way. The Judge told them quite bluntly that all deserters would be killed.

The Squire addressed the assembled villagers, many of whom were still arguing among themselves. He reminded them how bloodthirsty their enemies had been in their crimes, and what terrible atrocities they had committed in cold blood, and upon children, and so he worked their anger up to fever pitch.

'This should be good for a few of their necks!' shouted one villager, waving his scythe.

'It'll be a right massacre!' said another, with a mixture of fear and delight.

'Three muskets? Could you muster no more?' said the Squire, with disappointment, to a farmer who had come to help from a neighbouring village.

'Your guns will be no use 'gainst the devil,' put in a doom-merchant among the villagers.

'Are you one of his party?' yelled the Squire, with fury.

'I? No, sir, to be sure,' said the villager, backing down.

A woman called out from among the crowd, pushing herself forward.

'My daughter's up there!' she cried. It was Mistress Lucy Rogers, the mother of Winsome. 'You won't shoot my daughter?!'

'Her daughter be a ruddy witch!' came another cry.

'If anyone wants to take the law into their own hands,' warned the Squire, 'it will be very much the worse for them. They shall have me, and his lordship, to answer to.'

Through all this the Judge stood, brooding and silent, like a figure of doom. He had now heard new reports, and feared that he had greatly underestimated the numbers and power of his enemy. Many apparently reasonable villagers had, out of fear or for some other private cause, subscribed to, and soon become caught up in, the rituals of Angel Blake. Once they had taken part in these rituals, they could never leave. Angel had developed a deadly authority, and in everything she said, she spoke as if with the voice of another, more powerful, being. They grew to believe in her totally, and that through some supernatural skill, she knew all the answers, and would save them all.

The Judge had sensed that the time was ripe for him to return to the village, but he had not realised just how accurate his instinct had proved to be, nor how dangerous the situation had become. He now knew that if he had delayed, even for another day, the effect of that delay would have been disastrous.

Seeing the difficulty that the Squire was having in bringing the villagers to order, the Judge decided now was the moment to unveil his secret 'magical' weapon. He made a sign to his men, and at once they went to fetch the Crusader's Sword from its resting place in the luggage hold of his great coach. It was clothed in a ceremonial pall, like a church cross on Good Friday, and because of its shape, that was what it appeared to be. It was also extremely heavy, as could be seen when it was passed from hand to hand. Lit by flaming torches, because by then it was growing dark, the revealing of the sword was a fine piece of theatre, and the squabbling villagers were stunned into silence by it. As the pall fell away, the steel glinted. It put the fear of God into everyone, but it also gave them courage. Amazed by the way the villagers were now prepared to follow this awe-inspiring religious symbol with no argument, the Squire asked the Judge if the time had come.

'Shall we go, sir?' he said.

'So, we are ready,' said the Judge, looking around at the whole company. He then addressed them all.

'I pray you take note. If any man break ranks – either now or later – he shall pay for it dearly. Only the most strict discipline will save us in our hour of trial. Let those who are not resolved remain behind! Light the torches!'

The remaining torches burst into flame and were spread out among the group. The Judge gave orders for the Crusader's Sword to be covered once again, but kept close by him, as the company formed a thin line and moved stealthily forward into the woods.

Ralph had heard the preparations being made at the farm, and then had listened as the voices died away. Now from the one small window, low to the floor beneath the sloping roof of his hiding place, he could see the torches of the Judge's men and his small army of villagers winding in a line through the trees on the hill opposite. He felt he should be with them, had not his leg crippled him, but he knew that he would have been in great danger from them had they seen his leg, and he also knew how narrowly he had escaped discovery.

It was only when the glimmering lights had disappeared into the woods, and he felt completely secure from the hunt, that Ralph began to grow aware of his surroundings. Slowly it dawned on him what it meant to be in the very room where Rosalind Barton had been driven mad, and where Mister Peter had lost his hand. He had an overwhelming sense that something terrible had happened in this room, not only just recently, but hundreds of years ago, and this linked it to the chapel where he had found Cathy lying dead, and also to the creature which he had unearthed in Tarrant's Field.

He became aware of a smell, something between the odour of an old billy goat and that of rotting flesh. It seemed to emanate from beneath the floorboards. He remembered that he had first smelt that foul odour on his ploughshare in Tarrant's Field. He had not paid so much attention to it then because what he saw was far more alarming, but now it meant more to him, and it suggested that there was a presence in the room with him. The beast was there. He began to sense that he was being watched by the same eye that had looked at him from the broken skull in the ground. That same lidless eye was following him now wherever he went, even though he could not see it. His instinct was to protect his afflicted leg from its gaze. It was trying to induce fear in him, but he was determined to resist it, knowing that not just his life, but the lives of others, depended on him.

He kept his own eyes closed and tried to replace his fears with the memory of Cathy running along the field's edge on that sunny day, calling out his name. For a short while this gentle, calming image won through and remained uppermost in his mind, but all the time he could hear the old devil hobbling towards him to reclaim his leg.

Eventually the atmosphere in the room became so oppressive that he could hold out no longer, and flung himself at the door, thinking only that he must escape. The door tried to hold him in, but he used all his force against it until it gave way. When he had broken through, some of the pressure left him and he felt himself to be back in the real world. He looked down the stairs that he had come to know too well, conscious that Ellen was down there somewhere in the kitchen, where he thought he might yet be safe. But as he tried to go down the stairs, his leg betrayed him. His whole calf with its coating of fur was like a lead weight. He tried to drag it with him, but he fell headlong. The eye was still watching him as he fell. He fell down a whole flight of stairs, then a second, then a third, and down more flights of stairs than there ever were in the house, and into darkness, where he lay motionless.

Ellen could hear the commotion outside in the stairwell, but at the same time there was a frantic banging on the door which led from the kitchen into the yard. Two young girls were out there, and they seemed in a terrible state. They were both covered in mud, and one had lost her forearm.

'Help us, please help us,' they cried. 'We done run away, but to be sure they are after us!'

Ellen helped them inside.

'Oh glory!' she said when she saw the state of the girl with the lost forearm. She was small and not in a fit state to speak. The other girl, who was taller and quite handsome, did most of the talking.

'My sister had the skin,' she said, 'and they found out and caught us.' She almost choked with tears as she told the story.

'They hacked off her arm,' she said, 'just to get at the skin that was on it.' Ellen was dumbfounded and hardly knew what to say. This was clearly the work of Angel's devil-worshippers.

'Please help us, Mistress Vespers,' repeated the girl.

It surprised Ellen that this girl knew her name, but before she could ask her how that was, the girl came with another question.

'Is Ralph Gower here?'

Ellen was shocked even more by this, but knew that she had to keep Ralph's presence a secret.

'No,' she said immediately. 'No, I an't seen him, not this whole day.' She worried that she had been overemphatic, because she was not sure if the girl believed her.

'Ralph is a good man,' said the girl. 'He told us if we were in real trouble we should go to you, Mistress Ellen, and you would help us.'

'What can I do?' said Ellen.

'We're famished,' said the girl. 'We'm been on the run all day.'

'Easily done,' said Ellen. 'You stay there. I'll get you something.' She went into her little pantry, looking for cheese and cold meat.

When she had gone, the girls looked at each other. The smaller girl was far less incapacitated than had at first appeared. While the other kept watch, she quietly closed the pantry door and turned the key.

It was a while before Ellen realised she had been locked in, and by that time the two girls had located Ralph's senseless body at the foot of the stairs and were dragging it out through the front door of the farm. Outside, some young men were waiting to help them with their task of carrying him off into the woods.

In his unconscious state, Ralph could hear Angel's voice calling to him.

'Come to me!' she said, and her call was echoed by Margaret,

'Thou shall sleep with Angel, and thou shall sleep with me!' He could also hear the voices of other girls, chattering and chanting, and tending to him and his wounds, gently tearing at his knee-length breeches and exposing and stroking the fur on his leg. The sensation was both lovely and ugly.

The Judge had finally reached a place in the woods where he could see his quarry. A warm light was flickering in the far distance. It appeared a fire had been lit within the chapel, and it glowed on the trees around. He gave the order to his men to douse their torches and be silent. In the silence he could hear music, singing, drumming and chanting coming from the distant chapel, and from people gathered around the standing stone. A ceremony was already taking place. He advanced quietly towards it, ordering his followers to spread out and form a great ring around the worshippers, so that none would be able to escape when the time came. The evil, as he had said, must be destroyed utterly, or it might spread like a disease throughout the countryside. He had the worshippers all in one place now, and this was his only opportunity. If he missed it, it would mean disaster. Those that carried weapons had them at the ready. No-one made a sound.

As many worshippers as could be gathered there were dancing within the ruined chapel walls. Others were outside, circling round the Currell Stone, or looking into the chapel. The sense of expectation among all the dancers was palpable. To a deceptively beautiful melody played on a rustic flute, and a gasp from the worshippers, Ralph was carried in, and laid gently on the ground in the inner circle, close to the fire, like an honoured guest. After a while Ralph opened his eyes and blinked, like a man waking from a sweet dream into an unknown world, staring about him in bewilderment at all the wild dancers and their crazed faces as they worked themselves into a frenzy.

A young woman slowly approached him, the elder of the two sisters who had recently visited Ellen. She was now wearing a long ceremonial robe, which she let fall from her shoulders, revealing that she was naked underneath. She carried a sharp knife, and, stepping out of her robe, she spun it about her naked body with great skill, dancing like a snake to the beat of the drums. Its sharp edges glinted in the light of the fire, forming shining circles around her waist. She then slid the knife seductively down her thigh and offered the hilt to Ralph. All his instincts told him not to take it, but his hand had already grasped it, even against his will. The girl continued her dance, watching him closely, showing by her gestures that he should cut his own leg with the knife. It now appeared that they intended that their final victim should make of himself a willing sacrifice.

And he himself wanted it. That was the strangest thing. He was overcome by the feeling that once he had cut away the moving skin on his leg, he would be free. It took enormous willpower, and all his plain natural stubbornness, for him to keep the knife away. The girl intensified her dance, stroking her body against him, running her own finger along the blade of the knife in anticipation. She sucked the blood from her fingertip. Almost without realising it, and having resisted for so long, Ralph allowed the knife to graze his own leg. He looked at his calf and saw blood trickling down it. At that same moment a shadow formed itself in the smoke from the fire, and a cry of fear and delight went up from the whole crowd. He was there. A deep voice spoke from the shadow.

'He has my skin!'

Angel Blake now appeared in white and flung herself into the soft dark arms of that shadow. Her Master was manifesting himself, here among them. Curling her in his arms he seemed to grow in size, and his hideous face began to appear out of the smoke. It was a face that seemed to alter its shape with the moving shadows, appearing differently to each observer. It formed itself into the same face that had grinned down at the Reverend Fallowfield from the stone carving on the church tower, and had looked every day at his parishioners, but now it was a hundred times more terrible. It was a face created from the ancient fears of the local tribes, long before the days of recorded history. It fed upon those fears, demanding from its worshippers ever greater sacrifices, so that it could grow and extend its power. Now their god was out for revenge and would not easily be appeased, although Angel Blake herself still felt safe in its arms, looking out on her followers and smiling. As soon as Ralph Gower was deprived of his leg, she knew her Master would be complete.

The Judge heard the cries go up, but told his men to keep their powder dry until he chose the exact right moment to attack. He was now close enough to look through the broken windows of the chapel, and he himself saw the shadow growing out of the smoke of the fire.

'The beast is there,' he murmured, and gave the order, 'Fire!'

There was a great shriek, as many of those outside the chapel were struck down by the gunfire. The group dancing around the standing stone were all slaughtered. Others were woken by the sound, including Isobel Banham, who had been in a trance until then, caught up in the chanting and the frenzy. The gunshots broke through all that like the shattering of a mirror, and suddenly she could see the darkness of the real world.

The Judge had arranged for three rounds to be fired, so that there was time to recharge their weapons, and this round had been the first. Those who had survived it panicked and tried to get into the shelter of the chapel but were repelled by those inside, and so became easy prey for the second round. As she staggered out through the chapel doorway, Isobel was aware there were shadows in the bushes, and as if in a dream she thought that she could see the shape of Nathan Mandeville there, come to rescue her.

'Fire!' came the order, and the second round rang out, after which a woman's voice cried out in pain,

'Nathan!'

There was an eerie silence now, as the Judge held up his hand to stop the firing of the third round. It disturbed him greatly to hear his own name called out like that. Only one person was likely to have known it and called to him.

He came out of hiding and walked alone towards the chapel. There was nobody alive outside the chapel walls. The bodies that were strewn about were mostly the old and the infirm, or those that had been badly crippled in giving their skin to the devil. The Judge prodded one or two with his stick to be sure they were dead. Then he turned over the body of a woman. It was Isobel. As he had suspected, it was she who had called out, and he felt sick inside.

The Judge was soon overcome by a terrible rage; rage at the perpetrators of such horror, rage that he had been forced into taking such extreme measures, rage even at himself, but most of all, rage at the vile demon of superstitious fear which ruled those within the chapel, the devil of Chapel Folding. He demanded that the Crusader's Sword be brought to him. He would wield it himself.

The people inside the chapel were unarmed and had little with which to defend themselves against their assailants, only their faith in the power of the Master. He would save them, they were sure. Those who had died clearly did not deserve saving.

The Judge came forward and placed himself in front of the Currell Stone, where he could clearly be seen by those in the chapel. He was not to be put off by the hideous growl from within. A torch was lit, and the great cross of the Crusader's Sword was revealed. The superstitious folk inside the chapel were for a moment taken aback by the appearance of this powerful Christian symbol and let out a cry. Their terror was what the Judge had counted on.

Even Angel, at the shock of this apparition, parted from the arms of her Master. It was a fatal move, as it allowed her to experience a momentary doubt that her Master would in fact be able or want to save her. She had never saved others. All the fears which had been held back by the certainty that what she had done would be rewarded hundredfold reared up and flooded in on her. The flicker of a truly discordant thought came through to her, of the one mortal man for whom she had felt a kind of twisted love: her lost teacher, Lucian Fallowfield. Now that she had all the power and everything she had ever wanted, she was struck down by doubt, and the memory of her former life. A seed of uncertainty had been sown in her mind. She felt suddenly quite unprotected, and in a moment of desperate panic she leapt blindly out of the rough-hewn window of the chapel, fell and impaled herself on the pitchfork of Ned Carter, who was standing guard below. He had never thought, when he joined the crew, that such a thing might happen, and he pulled it back in shock. As he did so, others moved in with their home-made weapons to finish the job. It was hardly necessary. Angel had been pierced to the heart.

Once Angel had proved herself to be mortal, a great wave of fear overcame the other worshippers, who scrambled to escape from the chapel by whatever means they could, but they were trapped by the Judge's men. The Judge himself advanced towards the fire to meet in single combat the monster who crouched over it. With all his strength he whirled his sword around and flung himself into its movement as it cut deep into his shadowy opponent and thrust him down into the flames of the fire. Those flames leapt up, licking themselves around the old god in his raging, as it was believed the flames of hell had done long ago. The fire rose to the heavens, its sparks flying among the stars. The worshippers of the old god were on the run. The Judge was the Master now, and it was his demonic eye that held the devil in its power. Reason, will and mastery were the victors, and in his moment of triumph the Judge himself advanced into the flames to destroy the last remnant of his enemy.

What happened then, none knew nor saw. The villagers had fled, and the two opponents were alone within the chapel. Days later they examined the remnants of the fire. Of the supposed god or devil there was nothing to be seen or heard, nor was there any sign of the Judge. Some said that the Judge and the Master had become one at the moment of their death, others that the Judge had achieved a strange form of martyrdom. Others, such as Ned Carter, that great weaver of tales, claimed that Nathan Mandeville was still alive and would return someday.

What is recorded in the annals is that, following the conflagration, a miracle occurred. Those survivors, including Ralph Gower, whose bodies had been invaded by the Devil's Skin were instantly cured. The skin fell away from them, and their wounds vanished.

Rosalind Barton was also there among the surviving worshippers, having walked all the way to the chapel from the asylum, and when the miracle occurred, she painfully began to regain her sanity. She was reunited with her Peter and went to live in London in a quiet street, where Chapel Folding could be forgotten, except in her nightmares. It was only at the very end of her life that she confessed to what had happened in her youth.

It was as if the devil and his skin had been a dark fantasy in the minds of the villagers, and nothing more. The Squire held open house for the survivors, regaling them with stories of his own achievements on that night of nights, when the devil was defeated.

By coincidence, or perhaps not so, a soft rain had fallen at that time, which, so it was said, had a great cleansing power, and thereafter few people made further mention of witchcraft, satanism or any such malpractices within the village. As best it could, Chapel Folding slowly regained its good name, but in doing so it was forgotten, and after a while even tourists who liked to visit sites of horror could not tell you where it had been. Nothing was heard of it until many years later, when a group of young people accidentally stumbled upon the ruined chapel and began to feel a presence there.

A Note on the Author

Robert Wynne-Simmons is a writer, composer and film director who has always enjoyed breaking new ground. He has written poetry, plays, radio plays, short stories and novels, but specialised for a number of years in writing and directing for film and television. His film on the theme of Irish folklore, *The Outcasts* (1982), won eight international awards. More recently his career as a composer has come to the fore, with a symphony, song cycle, opera and the musical *The Gothic Game*.

A Note on the Illustrator

Richard Wells is an illustrator and graphic designer. He has provided graphic props for the likes of *Poldark*, *Sherlock*, *Doctor Who* and the recent BBC adaptation of Bram Stoker's *Dracula*. Outside of his television work, he makes and sells his own darkly folkloric artwork, often lino cut and printed by hand. He is the editor and illustrator of folk horror anthology *Damnable Tales*.

Unbound is the world's first crowdfunding publisher, established in 2011.

We believe that wonderful things can happen when you clear a path for people who share a passion. That's why we've built a platform that brings together readers and authors to crowdfund books they believe in – and give fresh ideas that don't fit the traditional mould the chance they deserve.

This book is in your hands because readers made it possible. Everyone who pledged their support is listed below. Join them by visiting unbound.com and supporting a book today.

Guy Adams
ADW Decorators
  (Lancaster)
Shaun Aitcheson
Gordon Aitken
Andreas Akerlund
Patrik Åkerman
David Aldridge
Adam Alexander
Ashley Allen
Darren Allen

Alokavira
Cleo Andriola
Taylor Andriotis
Bernard Angell
Richard Angliss
David Annandale
Michael Arnzen
A Astle
Tom Atkinson
Michael Awdry
James Aylett

Hunter B.
Duncan Bailey
Daniel Bairstow
Chris Baker
Peter Bakewell
Jason Ballinger
Neil Barham
Andrew Bark
Simon Barnard
Lauren Jane Barnett
Kevin Barnsley
David Barraclough
Jack Barrie
Rebecca Baumann
Joshua Baumgartner
Adam Baylis-West
Rosemary Baylis-West
Matthew Beaird
Joshua & Gabriel Bell
Richard Bennett
Lily Bentley
Benoit Beraha
Lucy Beth
Shana Bilbrey
Matthew Bintcliffe
Birdman & Artboy
Angie Birkett
Steve Birt

John Bishop
Chris Bissette
Kate Blackthorne and
    Melissa Holton
George Blandino-Ripley
Ann Bloxwich
Graham Blunt
Rob Bodger
Corey Bond
David Bone
Charley Bonnet
Craig Bowkley
Elizabeth Bradley
Paul Bradshaw
Andrew Brand
Derren Branson
Jason D. Brawn
Lyle C Briggs
Marc Bright
Matthew Bright
Jeff Brinkman
Scott Broadfoot
Andrew Brooks
Emma Brown
Jeff Brown
Eric Bruce / Weirdo
    Wonderland
Gary Budden

Jesse Bullington

Michael Buote

Stephen Burnette

Kevin Burns

Alan Byron

Paul Cadden

Joseph Camilleri

Ben Campbell

Jonny Campbell

Elion Caplan

Cara and Davie 31/10/22

DC Carlile

Jonathan Carr

Johnny Carrington

Lyndsey Catchpole
   Amanda Tivey

Cerise Cauthron

Inge Cederberg

Michael Cerliano

Adam Cesare

Barbara Chamberlin

Ryan Chani

Jamie Chappell

Rachael Chappell

Darren Charles

David Chrichard

Jared Christensen

Sean Kelly Christensen

Mitch Cichella

Snowcat Cinema

Chester Civelli

Chad Clady

John Clark

Jenny Clarke

Brandon Clauser

Gina Collia

Paul Colnaghi

Marc Comley

Harriet Connides

William Connors

Joleen Contillo

Charlotte Coombs

Ashley Cope

Alex Corbin

Gary Cossins

Donal Cox

Jason Creighton

Brenda Croskery

Alasdair Cross

Jack Arthur Cross

Katherine Crouch

Anthony Crutch

Helen Culyer

Peter Cumiskey

Mark Dakin

Bruce Davidson

Chris Davies
Layton James Davies
Jeremy Shane Davis
Laura Davis
Simon Davis
Celia Deakin
Clare Dean
Shaun Dean
Alex Delap
Steve Dempsey
Moira Dennison
Matthew Dew
Robert Dex
Fabiana Di Renzo
Cara Dixon
Harry Dobermann
Mark Dodyk
Dave Dow
Jennifer Draper
Tom Drayton
Thomas Drummond
William Dunn
Alice Durose
Tony Earnshaw
Adrian Elder
James Ellefson
Caitlin Elliman
Patrick Elliott

Marc Ellison
Robert Ellmer
Chris England
Liam Entwistle
Robert Espy
John Eternal
Alison Evans
David Evans-Powell
James Ewing
Paul Fannan
Nigel Farr
Jane Farrell
Jules Fattorini
Steve Fenton
Chuck Ferreira
Stace Fiendish
Hannah Filipski &
    Meghan Shearer
Matthew Finn
Victoria Finney
Andy Fish
Colin Fisher
Trevor FitzSimons
    Erlacher
Nicholas Flower
Brian Flynn
For RF
Stuart Forbes

Matthew Ford

Philip France

Rachel Francis

Richard Francis

Richard Freeman

Joe Fritsch

Matthias Fuchs

Michael Galley

Majda Gama

Craig Gardiner

Malcolm Gaskill

Deborah Gatty

Bret Gaunt

Christopher Gibson

Claudia Glazzard

Richard Gnosill

Jason Gomez

Jovi Gonyea

Jonathan Goodwin

Michael Goodwin

Christopher Grau

Stephen Graves

Jon Gray

Mark Gray

Sage Gray

Shauna Gray

Al Green

Darren Green

Kevin Greer

Damien Griffin

Ray Griffiths

Stephen Griffiths

Tim Gripton

Richard Gropp

Paul Guest

Ishani Guha-Shepherd

Mary Anne Guy

Carrie Haar

Simon Hagberg

Andy Hale

Joel J Hall

Lola Haller

Kim Halliday

Stephen Hampshire

Mathias Hansson

Jonathan Hargreaves

Katie Harper

Rob Harrigan

Matthew Harrington

Sagan Harris

Kate Harrison

Neil Harrison

Daniel G. Harvey

Laurence R. Harvey

Jo Haseltine

Glen Hattersley

Lindsay Headlee

James Hedges

Brendan Heldenfels

Perran Helyes

Spencer Hemming

Matt Henshaw

Stuart Herkes

Ben Hewitt

Tim Hicks

Richard Higgins

Richard Higson

Duncan C. Hill

James Hoare

Michael-Jason Hobbs

Amy Hoddinott

Jens Hoenscheid

Wayne Hollis

Mary Holmes

Bob Honey

Mark Hopwood

Eric Horstman

Andy Horton

Matthew Hoskins

Rhys Howell

Ian Howlett

Stephen Hubbard

Deborah Louise Hudson

Jennifer Hughes

Simon Hugo

Leon Hunt

Philip Hunt

Adrian Hunter

Ian F Hunter

Rowan Hunter

Tom Huxley

Kaye Inglis

BaT Jackson

Jason P Jackson

John Jacobs

Andrew James

Kier-La Janisse

Jackie Jardine

Krystian Jarosz

Paul Jenner

Christopher M. Jimenez

Tristan John

Graeme Johnston

Miranda Johnston

Chris Jones

Gareth Jones

Helen Jones

Jaime Jones

Kaz Jones

Mark Jones

Dr K

W K

River Kahrhoff
Milan Karol
Jonathan Kelly
Tony Kelly
William Kelly
Bradley Kelsey
Helen Kemp
Dan Kenny
Aaron Kent
John Keyes
Jon Kiefert
Dan Kieran
George F Killgoar III
J. Todd Kingrea
Jeff Kocan
Andrew Kolovos
Hendryk Korzeniowski
Matthijs Kouw
C. Kuhn
Jake Kulkowski
John Kyriacou
Dillon L.
Joshua Lagle
Alastair Laing
Andrew Lake
Richard Lansdall-Welfare
Ali Larkin
Zora Lassen

Emma Law
Eoin Lawlor
Eric J. Lawrence
Stephen Laws
Enda Leaney
Frazer Lee
Gavin Lees
Luke Lehane
Rob Letts
Johan Leuris
David Lewis
Huw Lewis
Librarian of the Occult
Jonathan Light
Amy Lloyd
Gareth Lloyd
Graeme Lockheart
Beatrice Rose Locock-
    Jones
Jon Long
Iain Lowson
William Lumsden
Paul Lyman
Theo MacGregor &
    Jerrold Oppenheim
Mark MacKintosh
Adam Macqueen
Jay Mahone

Phil Mahoney

Paul Mainon

Paul Male

Cheryl-Lynne Mansell

Clint Mansell

Marie-Jose and Maike

Beverley Martin

Jack Martin

Andrew Martyn

Glenn Masson

Wallace McBride

Yvonne Carol McCombie

John McCorkindale

Ian McDonald

Glen McFerren

Daniel McGachey

Geoff McHugh

Joe McIntyre

James McKinley

Patrick McKitrick

Tony McKormack

Haley McLoughlin

Danny McMonagle

Stephanie McNeil

Rory McSweeney

Arran Meachim

Sarah Meadows

Ian Merchant

Jason Merries

Matthew Michael

Michael Middleton

Mr. Midian

Frank Miles

Helen Miller

Richard Miller

Alex Mills

Francesca Milton

Neill Milton

Dan Mitchell

John Mitchinson

Lindsay Miyamoto

Deborah Moffat

Christopher Moon

Cevin Moore

Neil Moore

Stephen Moore

Elizabeth Morant

Hugh Morgan-Platt

Gary Moring

Rowena Morley

Beth Morris

Dale Morris

Michael Mortimer

Chloe Morton

Chris Mulholland

Linda Muller

Steve Mumford

Will Munday

Ellie Munro

Caroline Murakami

Nathalie Murcott

Euan Murray

Peter Murray

Benjamin Myers

Carlo Navato

Dave Neal

Adrian Neesam

David Neesam

Klil H. Neori

Paddy Newman

Andrew Nicholas

Babs Nienhuis

Phil Nobile Jr.

Candace Nola

Miriam Nolting

Stew Norriss

Ashley Novak

Karl O'Brien

Rodney O'Connor

Nigel O'Donnell

Penn O'Gara

Old Olaf Fowles

Richard Onslow

Jemma Orme

Dr Mark J Osborne

George Ospina

Kevin Paish

Michael Paley

Adam Park

James Parker

Scott Parker

Steph Parker

Toni Parker

Edward Parnell

Martin Parsons

Callum Paterson

James Paterson

Jordan Peach

Lisa Pearce Collins

Oliver Pearcey

Jared Pease

Joseph Jude Peecock

Francesca Pellatt

Anna Pembrey

Julian Pepper

Amy Peters

Joe Pettit

Leigh Phillips

Sophie Phillips-Jones

Maria Pickering

Charles Pieper

Andrew J Pine

Lance Pix

Catherine Plant

Kristin Plant

Justin Pollard

Will Poulter

Nick Powell

Gary Prange

Vineeth Pratheepan

Charles Prepolec

Ron Prescott

Ben Prior

Jon Quail

Philip Quail

Ray Radford

Christopher Rasmussen

Webberly Rattenkraft

Stephen Rawlinson

Gwenifer Raymond

James Reece

Alex Reed

Jerry Reed

Kris Rees

Josh Reynolds

Josh Reynolds Yeo

Robert Ribar

Elizabeth Richards

Jeremy Allen Riedel

Jamie Righetti

Shaun Riordan

Lukas Ritzel

Ian Roberts

Andrew Robinson

Rondal Robinson

Robert Jon Robison

Lee Robson

Margarida Rocha

Kenn Roessler

Ren Rogers

Frank Rooney

Paul Rooney

Gabriele Rossanese

Adam R Rosser

Mark Routledge

Stephen Routledge

Chris Rowell

Melissa Rung-Blue

Josh Saco

Lorenzo Sassi

Sophie Sawicka-Sykes

Tjark Schöneck

William P. Schumacher

Ben Scott

Carlson Scott

Christine M. Scott

Gemma Scott

Isla Scott

Emma, Freddie & Paul
    Scrivens
Kevin Segall
Chris Senior
Michael Seyfert
Dr S Shapland
Martin Sharkey
Onyx Sharp
Christopher Shaw
Graeme Shaw
Mary Elizabeth Shaw
Simon Shaw
Steve J Shaw
Matthew Shearin
Reece Shearsmith
Jacob Shell
Hilary Shenton
Richard and Linda
    Sheppard
Jim Shorter
Thea Shortman
Topi Siera
Silhouby
Christian Simcock
Rob Simmons (no relation)
Alan Sims
Andrew Slater
Edmund Slater

Mark Slater
Iain Smedley
Alan C Smith
Michael Smith
Rachel Smith
Simon Smith
Claire Solanki
Soror Somnia Clare
Stephen Sowerby
Aaron Speight
Adam Spellicy
Joe Spence
Izaak Spicer
Ross Spratt
Henry St.Leger
Justin Stanton
Roy Starling
Clare Stebbings
Sean Steele
Amanda Stefaniuk
Alistair Stevenson
Josh Stonehouse
Alistair Strachan
Aidan Strange
Andrew Stuart
Rachel Stuart
Chad Sutter
Nick Swift

Francis Taaffe
Gary Tate
Anne-Marie Taylor
Michael Taylor
Troy Taylor
Sam Terroni
Guy Thomas
Jack Thomas
Joshua Thomas
Billy Thompson
Helen Thompson
Chris Thorndycroft
Nick Thorpe
Ellee Thunfeldt
Dave Tighe
Matthew Tilt
Fiona Tims
Joanna Tindall
Tom Tokley
Keith Tomlinson
Rebecca Traynor
Anthony Treadwell
Carly Tremayne
Bill Trevett
Daniel S Turner
Frank L Turner
Jonathan Turner
Paul Turner

Daniel Underdown
Michael Upton
Anthony Vacca
Hilje van Beijnum
Joost van den Ossenblok
Kimberly Van Munching
Jente Vandormael
Shane Varley
Gary Veirs
Darrin Venticinque
Neil Vidler
Graham Vincent
Vlad
James Voller
Vulpine
Richard Wainman
Martyn Waites
Alan Wallace
Jim Waller
Phillip Walmsley
Julie Walton
Mark Wandra
Mark Wardecker
Stephanie Wasek
Craig & Julie Watkins
Derek Watson
Ange Weeks
Linda Westman

James Whelan
Laura White
Dan Whitehead
Kit Whitfield
Roger Whittington
Cameron Widen
James Wilde
Paul Wilde
Andrew Wileman
Daisy Wilkes
Joy Wilkinson
Arnold Williams
Bri Williams
Neil Williams
Owen Williams
Sian Williams
Zoë-Elise Williamson
Reuben Willmott

Brian Wilson
Derek Wilson
Jack Wilson
Robbie Wilson
Alisdair Wood
Lucy Wood
Janina Woods
John Woodward
Renick Wooley
Richard Woollard
Ian Woosey
Dorian A Wright
Tony Wright
Rob and Michelle Wyatt
Ewelina Wylub
Ben Wynne-Simmons
Georgia Young